NERVES OF STEEL

NERVES OF STEEL

Storybook written by

Fiona McHugh

Based on the CBC TV series produced by
Sullivan Entertainment

WIND AT MY BACK

HarperCollins*Publishers*Ltd

NERVES OF STEEL
Storybook written by Fiona McHugh

Based on the CBC TV series produced by Sullivan Entertainment with the
participation of Telefilm Canada and with the assistance of the Canada
Television and Cable Production Fund - License Program and with the
assistance of the Government of Canada Canadian Film or Video
Production Tax Credit.

Based on the books *Never Sleep Three in a Bed* and *The Night We Stole the
Mountie's Car* by Max Braithwaite.
The characters and incidents portrayed are entirely fictitious. Any
resemblance to any person living or dead is coincidental.

Wind At My Back is the trademark of Sullivan Entertainment Inc.
Teleplay "A Family of Independent Means" written by Janet Maclean and
Avrum Jacobson

http://www.harpercollins.com/canada
http://www.sullivan-ent.com/canada

First edition

Canadian Cataloguing in Publication Data

McHugh, Fiona
Nerves of steel

Based on the Sullivan Entertainment/CBC-TV series, Wind at my back.
ISBN 0-00-648154-X

I. Title.

PS8575.H78N47 1997   jC813'.54   C97-930249-8
PZ7.M478632Ne 1997

97 98 99 ❖ WEB 10 9 8 7 6 5 4 3 2 1
Printed and bound in the Canada

CHAPTER ONE

Fat saw the cop car first. It squealed to a stop in the street below just as he stepped out onto the balcony of his mother's rooming house apartment. He hadn't been expecting a cop car. He'd been expecting a taxi with his Aunt Grace inside. She was due to pick him and his big brother Hub up any minute and take them back to their Grandmother Bailey's home in New Bedford. Now that their mother was living in North Bridge, the boys were only allowed to visit her every other weekend. Those weekends were what they looked forward to most. They usually flew by. Always, as

the time to leave grew closer, Fat prayed his Aunt
Grace would be late. Maybe then they'd miss the
bus back to New Bedford and get to stay one more
night with their mother! But today, as he watched
the door of the cop car swing open and a burly
cop climb out, Fat felt he'd give anything to be as
far away from North Bridge as possible. He
stepped back from the railing. He could have
sworn that the cop looked straight up at him. Fear
smacked him, hard as the back of a hand on the
side of his head. Had the cop come for him? What
had he done? Cops meant trouble, he knew that
for sure. He prayed that this one wouldn't come
knocking at his mother's door. Another man got
out of the car and followed the cop to the front
door, but Fat didn't wait to check him out. Turning from the dusty balcony, he stepped quickly
back into the apartment.

He wished Pal were here with him now. Dogs
always made you feel better. He sat back down at
the table, feeling sick, bracing himself for the
knock on the door.

"So?" Hub said, staring at him. "Is she there or
not?"

Jeez. Aunt Grace. He'd clean forgotten about
her. What if Aunt Grace saw the cop? What if she
said something to Grandmother Bailey?

"What's up, Fat?" His mother was staring at him too.

His Mom was the only person Fat knew who could do a whole bunch of things really well all at the same time. Now her entire attention seemed fixed on him, but her hands kept right on folding his socks and packing them neatly in the battered suitcase he shared with his brother. Every so often, without missing a beat, she'd turn to stir the soup simmering on the stove. Her "nothing soup," she called it, because she made it out of almost nothing.

"What is it, pumpkin?" she asked again. "Come on, Fat, spit it out."

But just then a sharp rat-a-tat-tat struck the door. His Mom turned to answer it.

"Honey Bailey?" The male voice sliced through the airless room.

"Yes?" His mother sounded far away, subdued.

Fat forced himself to look over at the cop. But the cop wasn't there. Instead a gray man filled the doorway. Gray hat, gray hair, gray suit. A gray leather briefcase peeked meekly out from under one drab arm. Where did the cop go?

"I represent North Bridge Savings and Loans," the man said tonelessly. "This property's been taken over by us since your brother skipped town."

"Look," his Mom said quickly. "I'm in a hurry. Someone's picking my kids up any second now. I don't have time to—"

"You're Joe Callaghan's sister, ain'tcha?" The man in the suit was growing irritable.

"Yes, but—"

"Ain't he the former landlord here?"

"Yes, but—"

"Ain't you been sharing this apartment with him for quite a while now?"

"I had to move in here, after my husband died. I had no choice—" His mother's voice cracked.

Hub rose slowly to his feet. Fat could tell he wanted to smack the guy.

"Look, I don't give a tinker's curse about your personal affairs, Mrs. Bailey. All I wanna know is do you or do you not intend to go on paying the rent?"

"Of course I do!"

Something white rustled in the man's hand. He thrust it at her. It looked official.

"In that case, this letter serves to inform you, and all other remaining tenants, of a monthly rent increase. Effective the first of September."

Their mother caught her breath. She blinked down at the letter as though it were written in secret code.

"I'll be back at the end of the month," droned the man in gray. "Any tenants behind in their rent will be escorted off the premises ... by my buddy here."

He stepped back, and the hair on Fat's neck stood up. Behind the gray man, like a navy-blue shadow, stood the cop.

"You won't be escorting *me* anywhere. This apartment is paid up till the end of the month, and you'll get your increase on time." Honey Bailey was furious. No constable was gonna drag her off the premises. Over her dead body.

After she slammed the door, Honey sank into a chair, the paper in her hand shaking. A quiet fell over the three of them. Fat was afraid to open his mouth in case tears came out instead of words.

Ever since his dad had died he'd had this ache at the back of his throat. Like he could never, ever cry enough to get rid of it. The way Fat saw it, when someone close to you died, someone who had no business up and dying on you like that, it was like the bottom falling out of your world. Everything you ever dreaded and never spoke of became possible. Even being separated from your mother and baby sister. Even cops coming to take you away.

CHAPTER TWO

Leaning back against the warm leather of the cab,
Grace Bailey tried not to worry. The sun shone. The
warm air drifted in through the rolled-down win-
dows. You should be singing, not fretting, she told
herself. There was a tune somewhere at the back of
her mind, a popular tune, one you could dance to.
But as the car turned on to her sister-in-law's street,
the worries refused to go away. She disliked taking
her nephews back to New Bedford after their
weekend visits to their mother. For the life of her,
she couldn't see why Honey should be separated
from her sons at a time when they needed her
most. That had been May Bailey's decision.

May had never warmed to her eldest son's wife,
never welcomed her into the Bailey family. It was
clear to Grace that her mother felt she had nothing
in common with her daughter-in-law. But now,
with Jack's death, they had a shared sorrow. Grace
had hoped it might bring the two women together.
But if anything, it seemed to have widened the rift
between them. With lightning speed Mrs. Bailey
arranged for Violet, Honey and Jack's two-year-old

daughter, to be sent to live with relatives. And she insisted that Hubert and Henry, as she called Hub and Fat, remain at her home in New Bedford, while making it perfectly plain to Honey that she was not welcome there.

Poor Honey. Instead of the comfort and support she deserved, she had been cast out of her husband's family to look for work on her own. And in the depths of the Depression, too, when jobs were as scarce as hen's teeth. It was hard for Grace to believe that her own mother could be so cruel and insensitive. It was almost as if she blamed Honey for Jack's death.

Through the windscreen of the cab, Grace caught a glimpse of two men climbing up the front steps of Honey's building. Shooting forward, she grabbed the back of the cabbie's seat. "Say, driver. Did you see what I saw?"

"Look, lady," the man eased the cab into a free space at the curb, "I keep my eyes on the road, see? That way nobody gets killed. You want me to guess what you seen, you pay me danger money."

Oh, go jump in a lake! she thought. She sighed and slumped back in her seat. One of the men she'd seen was a policeman, she was prepared to swear to that. The other? Darn it, the other looked just like a bailiff. Grace knew that Joe Callaghan, like countless other Canadians just then, was drowning in money problems. He had borrowed from Honey and done a bunk, leaving the bank to foreclose on his mortgage and Honey to pay the rent on the apartment all by herself.

Could those two men be on their way to harass her sister-in-law for money? Should Grace try to stop them? She reached for the door handle. Then hesitated. After all, what could she do to help? She had no money of her own to offer Honey. Much as she'd like to, she couldn't exactly summon the cavalry to Honey's aid.

"Hey, lady! You fixin' to pay me or what?"

She'd forgotten all about the cabbie.

"Oh my! Oh yes, I ... yes ..." she babbled, rooting around in her purse, her eyes fixed on the front door of the apartment building. Just as her fingers closed around a dollar bill, the cop and Mr. Gray-Suit emerged from the building and walked away. Grace stared after them, the bill dangling from her fingers.

"Lady?" The cabbie tugged at the bill locked in her grasp.

"Oh. Yes. Sorry, I ... No. No, wait!" She snatched the bill back. "You stay here, okay? I'll go fetch my nephews. Then you can drive us all to the bus."

"Which bus might that be?"

"Why, the New Bedford bus, of course."

"Better make it snappy. That bus don't wait for ditherers."

Oh, go soak your head, she almost snapped, but didn't.

With as much dignity as she could muster, Grace stepped out of the cab and headed for her sister-in-law's apartment.

A pale, shaky-looking Honey answered the door.

"Hello, there, Honey." Grace adopted her cheeriest manner. "Are those nephews of mine ready? We don't want to miss our bus."

Honey attempted a smile. "Sure, Grace. They're all packed and waiting. I just wish I could say they're raring to go."

Grace hated to watch her sister-in-law saying goodbye to those boys. Though Grace had never married and had no children of her own, she could still imagine what it must feel like to have to live apart from your kids. Honey always put a brave face on it, always smiled as she drew her boys to her and kissed them. But her pain was there, written on her face for anyone to read. Anyone with half a heart, that is.

"Bye, Mom." Poor little Fat looked so miserable Grace wanted to weep. After all, he was only ten years old!

When it was Hub's turn to hug his mother, Grace could see he was holding back tears. Looking up at her with those solemn eyes of his, he said softly, "Don't worry, Mom. We'll find jobs in New Bedford. We're gonna do our bit to get us all back together again."

His mother held him tightly. "I don't want you worrying your head about money, Hub. At least I've got my job. Maybe soon I'll be able to put some money by. Just you keep your chin up, okay, sweetie? You're the man of the family now. And I'm counting on you to keep an eye on your little brother."

Hub nodded, unconsciously squaring his shoulders. Though he was only twelve, he felt he was ready for the responsibility.

As soon as they were ready, Grace rushed the boys down to the waiting taxi.

"Better hold onta yer hats," the driver ordered. "If you wanna make that bus, I'm gonna have to stomp on the gas."

The car lurched forward, causing the three passengers in the back to fall against each other. At the sudden burst of speed, the boys' solemn expressions dissolved. Yelling their approval, they urged the driver on.

The knot in Grace's stomach loosened. A familiar melody started up again in her head. She wasn't normally the worrying kind. But since her brother's death she often felt overcome by the difficulties of the situation. *If only I had someone to talk to about all this,* she thought. Someone to advise me. Someone to watch over me. But was there anyone who spared a thought for her? Who knew how much she grieved for Jack, her favorite brother? Who appreciated how hard it was for her to live at home, doing her mother's bidding day after day? She couldn't think of a soul. Not one, single, solitary person—Wait a minute! She felt a light go on in her heart. There *was* someone! There was Judd Wainwright, her old flame from high school! She'd met him recently, by magic, by accident, on the bus to North Bridge. They'd talked and joked and laughed and it was as if all the years that had passed since they last spoke had never happened. Judd didn't see her as Mrs. Bailey's spinster daughter, she could tell. Judd saw her for who she was. And then it occurred to her: Judd Wainwright was a traveling salesman. A man who spent most of his time on the road. Judd Wainwright might very well be on their bus to New Bedford this afternoon!

Joy welled up in her. She had to swallow hard to stop herself from singing right out loud. Instead, she stretched out her arms and folded them about her nephews. The song she hummed softly was a hit of the day, lilting and dreamy. It made her feel like dancing. "There's a somebody I'm longing to see, I hope that he, turns out to be, someone to watch over me ..."

CHAPTER THREE

"You think Pal's gonna be waiting for us when we get home?" Fat asked Hub as they climbed onto the New Bedford bus.

His brother tensed. "It ain't home, Fat. It's Grandmother's house. Don't you go calling it home."

"I didn't mean it was *really* home. Like what we used to have. I just meant—when we get back, d'you think Pal will be there, at the bus stop, wagging his tail?"

"Sure he will. Unless he's run away again. C'mon. Let's sit here. You can have the window seat."

Fat climbed onto the seat and opened the window straight away. The next time he spoke, his voice was quiet. "You think we'll ever have a real home again, Hub?"

Hub put his arm around his younger brother. "Sure we will, Fat. We just gotta think of some way of earning money. That's what Mom needs right now, see? Enough money so she can afford a place for all f— ... all four of us. So we can all be together."

He was glad Fat wasn't looking at him. Because just then he'd almost said "all five of us." Stopped just in time. He'd never really thought too much about it before, but suddenly five seemed like such a neat, satisfying number. Two parents. Three kids. Just right somehow. Why did it have to get all messed up? Why did that cruel subtraction have to happen? Five take away one. Just like that. Fat was gazing out the window again, waiting for the bus to pull away, muttering something under his breath. Hub leaned closer. "Together," Fat was whispering, over and over, like a prayer. "Together. Together. Together. Together. Together ..."

Hub wondered if his Aunt Grace would notice. But she had snapped open her little silver compact and was busily powdering her nose. She seemed nervous, excited. She probably wanted to look her best for Grandmother, Hub decided. Grandmother was always nagging Aunt Grace about taking better care of her appearance, not letting her shoulders droop, wearing her gloves in public and on and on and on. Hub couldn't figure out why his aunt put up with it. Why didn't she fight back?

Grace must have felt him staring, because she looked over at him just then. "That policeman ..." she said abruptly.

Hub looked at her blankly. *Please God*, he thought, *don't let her ask about that cop.*

"Didn't I see a policeman going into the rooming house this morning?"

"You mean ... a cop?" Hub stalled. He sure didn't want Grandmother Bailey finding out about that cop. Who knew what cockeyed conclusion she might jump to. She'd probably accuse Mom of being some kind of criminal.

"Yeah ..." Grace eyed him levelly. "I guess that's another word for a policeman." Returning her gaze to the mirror, she licked her little finger and touched it daintily to her eyelashes. "Was there a problem?"

She had Fat's attention now, too. He was staring at his aunt, eyes wide with worry. Hub nudged him with his elbow, warning him not to answer.

"A problem ...?" he repeated stupidly, as if the word had just been invented. He had to think of something—some way to answer that wouldn't be a lie. But before he could say anything, he was saved by a booming voice from a last-minute passenger making his way down the aisle.

"Why, Grace Bailey," the passenger hollered. "This must be my lucky day. I was hoping I'd bump into you again."

Hub watched, fascinated, as a wave of pink crept up his aunt's neck and flooded her cheeks. There was a quick click and a gleam as the compact vanished into the recesses of her purse. She turned her head.

The cop, Hub could tell, had been eclipsed.

"Hello, Mr. Wainwright," his aunt replied, and it was almost a purr.

Judd had been heading towards them, but her greeting made him hesitate. He took his fedora in both hands. "Wainwright?" he queried, as though he'd never heard the name before. "Wainwright? Don't you mean 'Judd,' Grace? I thought our friendship entitled us to use first names. Especially after our last bus ride together!"

The blush in his aunt's cheek deepened to mauve. Judd seemed to notice her blush too, and take courage from it. Reaching into his jacket, he pulled something from an inside pocket and handed it to Aunt Grace with a flourish.

"Gum?" he offered.

He had quite a smile, Hub realized. It made you feel good just seeing it.

Aunt Grace smiled back. "Gee, thanks. Thanks a lot ... Judd."

She said his name as though she'd just stepped into the room to announce that dinner was on the table and it was going to be something delicious. A ham, maybe. Or a roast chicken. Something that suited a celebration.

When Judd heard her say his name like that he sat down beside her with a kind of thud. As though she'd whacked him with a broom. He looked at her in silence for a second, and then his smile shone out again, just like the sun. All three Baileys sat back and basked in it.

In Judd's cheerful company, Hub forgot all about his worries over his Mom and Violet and money. He even forgot his grief for his Dad. For a few hours he was a normal twelve-year-old again, laughing at Judd's tall stories, telling jokes, kidding around, feeling as though the weight of the world had suddenly lifted from his shoulders.

Before he knew it, the bus was pulling into the New Bedford station, stopping very close to where Grandmother Bailey stood with Uncle Bob, waiting for them.

Fat gave a yell and dashed out the door. He

had caught sight of Pal, straining at his leash, wagging his feathery tail and doing his best to break free from Uncle Bob's grasp. The dog was mostly collie, a beautiful golden color with a white chest and dark, floppy ears.

"Pal, hey Pal!" he cried, running over to stroke and pat the dog affectionately.

Erect and regal, May Bailey stood beside her only remaining son and watched as her grandson lavished his affection on the equally demonstrative Pal. She did not stoop to hug or kiss Fat. She did not even smile. "I'm glad to see that mother of yours sent you home in one piece," was all she said.

Hub's light heart turned over and sank.

"Home," she had called it. But it was no more home to him than any prison. And the way she said "that mother of yours" — as though she hated Mom. All his troubles flapped back, dark vultures settling on his shoulders. He felt like that guy, Atlas, Fat had told him about, the one who'd been condemned to carry the weight of the heavens on his back. And feeling that way, he sent up a prayer: *Help me make money, God. Help me get us out of this mess.*

As he stood by the empty bus, apart from the other Baileys, waiting for the suitcase he shared with Fat, Hub saw his grandmother's eyes fall on

Aunt Grace. She and Judd Wainwright were shaking hands, saying goodbye. The pink still hadn't faded from his aunt's cheeks and she looked pretty, Hub noticed. Pretty and very young, for all that she was over thirty years old.

But it was his grandmother's expression that held his attention. A look he recognized had come over her face. He'd seen it many times before: an angry, determined look that said, "All is not as I would like it, and something will have to be done!" It was a look Grandmother wore whenever his mother was around. But this time, it was directed towards poor Aunt Grace.

CHAPTER FOUR

His Majesty avoided Grace's eye.

Handsome, almost stern in profile, his averted gaze suggested disapproval. Grace yawned. It was late, and she was growing used to disapproval. What would His Majesty think of Judd, she wondered idly. Would his royal eye look kindly on the stout, awkward salesman whose very presence made her pulse race? Probably not. His Royal Highness would undoubtedly side with Mother.

Those in power tended to sympathize with others in power.

"Off with his head!" she muttered.

Picking up George the Fifth, she ripped the stamp away from the envelope and dropped it in a large basin of water.

"Take that, Your Majesty!" she growled. Most of Grace's stamps bore images of crowned and powerful rulers. Yet they had all ended up floating in Grace's basin, soaking their heads. Was there a lesson there for Mother, she wondered?

From the bulky sack by her chair, Grace pulled another handful of empty envelopes and began the whole process again.

She did not look up when her mother came into the dimly lit kitchen, her cane tapping against the flagged tiles. She waited, assessing her mother's mood.

"Look at this mess!" May Bailey complained. "Stamps in basins of water! Stamps on cookie sheets! Envelopes underfoot everywhere! Nothing but clutter and mess! Why you waste your time sending used stamps off to New Jersey I'll never understand, Grace."

Because you'll never bother to try, thought Grace to herself, keeping her head well down. Her hands continued to rip stamps off envelopes and dunk them in water. Once the remaining bits of envelope had loosened from the soaking stamps, she would lift them out and place them on cookie sheets to dry.

"Postage alone must cost you more than you earn from this absurd little business!"

"All right, so the stamp dealer in New Jersey pays me a pittance. At least I'm trying to earn my own income, Mother."

Darn it. Grace had to force her anger back down. Her mother knew exactly what words and tone to use to get her blood-boiling, rip-snorting mad. Grace almost admired her skill in the brutal art of baiting.

Mrs. Bailey savored her small victory for a moment before reminding herself that Grace's pathetic attempts to earn pin money were not the issue here. No, the bone Mrs. Bailey intended to pick with her daughter was a larger one. She would have to be careful how she proceeded. Strategy, she warned herself, was everything.

Biding her time, she moved slowly behind her daughter's chair and waited. After a few seconds, Grace began to whistle tunelessly, a sure sign that she was growing unnerved.

A grim smile lifted the corners of May Bailey's thin mouth. So far so good. She held her tongue some more. The tick of the kitchen clock and

Grace's whistle were the only sounds in the dimly lit room.

"You haven't said one word about your trip," Mrs. Bailey began at last, when she judged the time to be right. "You know I always like a full report."

Grace's whistling continued.

"I suppose Honey displayed her usual flair for bad behavior?"

The whistling stopped. May waited; Grace never could resist leaping to Honey's defense.

"Honey was fine," she said. "Her apartment's fine. So is her job. She's hoping she can start saving a little money very soon, so that she and the kids can get back together. That'll be just fine too, don't you think, Mother? Fine and dandy?"

Grace knew very well that Mrs. Bailey disliked the thought of her daughter-in-law making a go of things. But Mrs. Bailey had no intention of getting into a battle with Grace about Honey. What was at issue right now was Grace's heart. Her daughter's heart was in peril, and Mrs. Bailey intended to fight to save it. If she had to use devious tactics in the process, well, so be it. She'd been a successful business woman all her life, running the family mining company single-handedly after her husband died. She could get her hands dirty with the best of them.

The strategy May Bailey had selected for her campaign was one known to military experts as a feint. By mounting a sham attack, you could divert your opponent's attention from the real one. It also had the benefit of tiring your enemy, so that he or she was less well prepared when the genuine attack took place.

Grace yawned again and rubbed her eyes. It had been a long, eventful day. In the basin, the crowned heads of Europe were beginning to blur.

Mrs. Bailey readied herself for attack. If her strategy worked, Grace would never even know what hit her. But first she edged forward slightly, so she could read her daughter's face. Her own expressed nothing but concern.

"I have to admit, I'm a little worried about you, Grace," she began smoothly.

Grace looked startled. "About me, Mother?"

"Yes, my dear. All this traveling. It's so ... wearing."

Grace's tone softened. "It's late, Mother. Why wouldn't I be tired?"

"It's those bus trips, dear. They're too much for you. You can't keep up this sort of thing on a regular basis, you know. Escorting those boys down to North Bridge every two weeks. Dropping them off, coming back home again, then going back again by bus just to escort them home. It's a strain on your health, child."

Grace stirred the stamps in the basin with her index finger. Her eyes were fixed on her mother. Their expression was hard to read.

"Honestly? You're worried about my ... health, Mother?"

"Of course I am. Losing one child makes a mother all the more fearful of losing another. Besides, that bus is no place for a lady. Full of germs and riff-raff ..."

May's voice trailed off. She felt unstrung by Grace's stare.

"Riff-raff?"

"You know. The great unwashed. Common people. The loud and the vulgar."

Oh dear. Grace was on to her. She could tell.

"You saw me talking to Judd Wainwright. Is that what this is all about?"

The mere mention of that upstart's name caused May to throw strategy out the window. Once, way back when they were at high school together, Judd Wainwright had made a play for Grace. Her daughter had certainly been inter-ested in him then. But May had judged Judd unworthy and crushed the romance before it had time to bud. Now, somehow, Judd Wainwright, a blatant opportunist if ever she met one, had wormed his way back into her daughter's life. Perhaps even into her heart!

"Did you actually sit beside that man on the bus, Grace?"

"I happened to run into him, Mother. It was an accident."

"He just materialized, did he? Out of thin air? A man his size? Sounds like a scientific miracle to me."

"Yes, wasn't it?" Her sarcasm was lost on Grace, whose tired face had relaxed into a radiant smile.

That smile decided May Bailey. To hell with strategy. She was in charge. Willing or unwilling, her daughter would obey.

"There will be no more miraculous meetings. Do you hear me? From now on you will drive the boys to North Bridge by car."

"But Mother! You *know* I can't drive!"

"You will learn. As long as you're living in my house, under my roof, you will obey my rules. Do you understand?"

Grace's eyes were on the stamps. In the somber light her face looked gray and shadowed. "Yes, Mother."

"Good. Now tidy up these ridiculous stamps and get to bed."

CHAPTER FIVE

Bright and early the next morning, Mrs. Bailey hustled Grace out to the car and into the driver's seat. Then, as quickly as her arthritic legs could carry her, she clambered in beside her daughter. The car was large and imposing, cream-colored with a brown roof.

"Place your right foot on the brake and your left on the clutch. So ..." Seizing Grace's left ankle, she steered it towards the clutch. "Is your right on the brake? Good. Sit up straight, for heaven's sake. Are you ready?"

Grace was very pale. She held onto the steering wheel as though she were drowning.

"Well? What are you waiting for? Start the car."

Grace's hands tightened around the steering wheel. Mrs. Bailey prized them open.

"Turn the key and start the ignition." She spoke slowly, as if speaking a foreign language.

Grace stared at the dashboard. Gingerly, she switched the key to the right and pressed the starter button. The Ford leapt forward, swerved and stalled.

May Bailey readjusted her hat. She looked at her daughter in disgust. "You can't accelerate and brake at the same time, Grace. Don't you know *anything* about the laws of physics? Now do it again. Properly this time."

This time Grace forgot to put in the clutch. The engine scraped and screamed. So did May Bailey.

"The clutch! Dammit, Grace, what did I tell you about the clutch?"

"I can't do it, Mother. I want to, honest I do. But I can't. Why do you insist on putting me through this torment?" A tear trickled down Grace's cheek.

May's impulse was to shriek in exasperation, but she reminded herself of the perils awaiting her daughter on the bus. Controlling herself, she modified her tone.

"Of course you can do it, dear. Ease up gently on the clutch while at the same time, the *same* time, Grace, pressing slowly, *slowly* on the gas. There. Yes. See? That's not bad, dear. Not bad at all."

The Ford inched down the driveway and out into the street.

Grace gulped. They were moving. Crawling might be a better word for it, it's true, but they *were* on the move. She hoped her mother wouldn't make her go any faster. A snail's pace was way too fast for her. She dreaded shifting gears.

"Accelerate, silly! Not *too* much! Shift gears, go on!"

If only Mother would pipe down! Grace pretended not to hear.

Just as another car approached them, May leaned over and shifted the car into second gear herself. In doing so she bumped against her daughter, who swung the steering wheel widely.

"Merciful heavens, are you trying to get us killed?" May yelled, both hands clutching her hat.

But Grace paid no attention. She was, she felt, getting the hang of things. What was all the fuss about? Driving was a cinch! With a grand gesture, she swung the wheel in the opposite direction, missing an oncoming car by inches and threatening to mow down a passing pedestrian. "What's that booby doing in the middle of the road?" she demanded in outrage, then clapped a hand over her mouth with a horrified giggle. She was, she realized, beginning to sound just like Mother.

May Bailey closed her eyes. For an instant she considered stopping the car, changing seats with Grace and driving home. Her Ford was her pet, her plaything, her pearl of great price. The very idea of it suffering a dent or scratch filled her with pain. But then she thought of Judd Wainwright and knew there was no going back.

"Change into third at once, Grace," she snapped, opening her eyes.

For a while they drove in silence. Her brush with the pedestrian had dampened Grace's confidence. But gradually, as no further mishap occurred, her courage returned. Her grip on the steering wheel relaxed and she began, tentatively, to enjoy herself.

By now they had left the town behind. The road curved through woods dense with spruce, fir and cedar. It was cooler here, the air scented with the tingly, spicy smell of cedar. A sense of release wafted over Grace.

She knew very well that her mother's decision to teach her to drive was a ploy—a ploy to keep her off the bus and away from Judd Wainwright. This insight fanned to life the flame of resentment that had been smoldering inside her ever since she was a little girl. The trouble was, her life was never her own. Her mother interfered and manipulated whenever she saw fit. Who knows, if her mother hadn't poked her nose in years ago, Grace might very well have been Mrs. Judd Wainwright by now. But an idea was forming in her mind. The car might be her key to freedom! After all, she'd been begging for driving lessons since she was eighteen but her mother had always refused, claiming Grace was much too clumsy to learn. Well, by golly, she *would* learn. She'd grab this chance with both hands. She'd learn to drive and she'd keep on driving. As far away from Mother as she could get.

Now, as she drove uncertainly along the road hemmed with trees, Grace felt like singing with sheer exhilaration. She'd drive everywhere. Up hill and down dale. Over the hills and far away. Until one day, she'd bump into Judd again. He'd be striding along a road just like this one, and she'd be driving by in her best motoring hat, the one with the cherry-colored lace. He'd see her, glance at the car, take in the fact that she was driving. Sweeping his hat from his head he'd smile that smile of his and he'd say ... and he'd say ...

"Grace!" Her mother shrieked. "The brake! GRACE!"

A tree. Oh, God. A massive tree loomed up out of nowhere. Grace yanked the steering wheel with all her might but it was too late. The tree smashed against the windshield with a sickening jolt. She heard the shattering of glass, and then the blaring of a horn.

Grace's head throbbed. She felt sick to her stomach, but at least she was all in one piece.

Cautiously, she shifted her head to one side. It hurt.

"Mother?"

In the passenger seat, her mother was slumped forward. She appeared to be sleeping.

"Are you all right, Mother?"

No answer. The blare of the horn continued. Blood oozed from her mother's forehead. Grace sat up quickly. The horn stopped. She'd been leaning on it the whole time.

"Answer me, Mother!"

Let this be a nightmare, Grace prayed, *please, please, God!"*

She reached for her mother, pulling her over, half into the driver's seat.

"Oh no. Mother. I wanted to escape from you. I never meant for you to get hurt! Please be all right!"

Cradling her mother in her arms, Grace sobbed like a child.

May Bailey was not to be defeated by anything as pedestrian as a car accident.

The impact of the collision had knocked her out. In addition to her concussion, she was bruised all over, and the wound in her head had caused her to lose copious amounts of blood. Grace got away with nothing more than a few aches and

pains. Luckily for both women, a local farmer had
witnessed the collision and driven them to the hospital in his horse and cart.

Mrs. Bailey would be fine, Dr. Barlow, her
physician, assured the family. She could leave the
hospital soon—but not quite yet. Dr. Barlow
wanted to keep an eye on her. Concussions could
be tricky, he explained to Aunt Grace. He wanted
to make sure there would be no lasting side effects.
A week, he said. At least a week.

Fat couldn't believe his ears. A whole week
without Grandmother! No bossing. No sarcastic
remarks. No silly, pointless rules. A whole week
with only Aunt Grace to keep an eye on them.
Jeez, it sounded like heaven.

As soon as he took stock of his grandmother,
however, he felt a twinge of remorse. She looked
mighty terrible, stretched out on the bed like a
long, white, lumpy sheet. She was still woozy
from being knocked out, he could tell. Her eyes
weren't focusing properly, which made her seem
kinder somehow.

But it was his Aunt Grace for whom he felt real
pity. Not counting his dad's funeral, he'd never
seen her so upset. Tears welled up in her eyes
whenever she looked at her mother. She blamed
herself for every single one of her mother's

injuries. Poor Aunt Grace was probably suffering from shock too.

"I just wasn't paying enough attention," she'd sobbed when they met her at the hospital. "I was lost in my own thoughts. Never saw that bend in the road. Never saw that dang-blasted tree, either, until it was coming straight at me. Oh, poor Mother!" She'd cried so hard, Hub had to hug her to make her stop.

"Grandmother had no business forcing Aunt Grace to drive like that!" Hub said later that night as he waited for Fat to finish brushing his teeth. "Dad always said driving a car's a huge responsibility. Not something you can pick up in one lesson."

"Maybe it's a good thing Grandmother's having her head examined." Fat spat into the basin. "Sounds like it needs an overhaul."

Chapter Six

By the second day after the accident, Aunt Grace had recovered enough to walk to the premises of the local newspaper. Under an arrangement she had made some time ago with Mr. Cramp, publisher and editor of the *New Bedford Weekly*

Chronicle, all stamped envelopes coming into the office were saved for her. At least once a week Grace carted home a huge load of envelopes, all destined to have their stamps ripped from them and packed off to New Jersey.

Fat would have preferred to stay home and listen to the radio, but Hub insisted that they both accompany Aunt Grace to the newspaper office. All Hub seemed to think about these days was finding a job, so he could earn money to give Mom. Fat wanted to help too, but he couldn't really believe anyone would give a job to two kids. Not when there were plenty of men and women desperate for work.

It turned out Fat was right.

"All my paper routes are full," Mr. Cramp explained, as he handed over a gigantic paper bag to Aunt Grace. "And most of my carriers aren't boys either. No sirree. They're full grown men."

"You *will* let them know if there's an opening, won't you?" Grace asked.

Instead of replying, Mr. Cramp let out a sudden yelp of pain. Staring down at the paper a young man had just handed him, he grasped his stomach as though in agony. Hub and Fat stepped back from his desk in a hurry.

"Didn't I tell you never, *ever* to say 'fairly

unique'?" groaned Mr. Cramp, massaging his belly as though the offending reporter had just kicked him there.

"I guess I...I must've forgot. Sorry, Mr. Cramp," the journalist stammered.

"Why can't you see?" grumbled Mr. Cramp. "It's either unique or it's not. And if it's not, why in heaven's name bother using the word?" He adjusted his pants gingerly. "Now my stomach's all in a heave! 'Fairly unique'! Oufff, revolting!"

Aunt Grace raised an eyebrow at the boys and they all tiptoed out of the newspaper office.

"You think that's why they call him Mr. Cramp?" asked Fat. "Cause he's always bellyaching?"

"Mr. Cramp's in love with the English language," answered Aunt Grace, who was searching through her wallet while trying to balance the bag of stamps and walk at the same time. "I guess not everyone has the same feeling for it."

"Here, let me." Hub took the bag from her. "I just wish he could've tried us out at least." He frowned down at the sidewalk. "How're we ever gonna help Mom if we can't earn some money?"

"I could let you in on my stamp-collecting business."

"Those people in New Jersey don't pay you nearly enough, Aunt Grace. It takes ages before you get paid, too. We need to find a serious job, paying serious cash right away."

"But thanks, anyway," Fat chimed in.

Grace smiled. She closed her wallet with a sigh. "Speaking of serious money, we'd better go see how Mr. Jefferson's doing with Mother's car."

Down at the garage, Hub tried his best to talk Mr. Jefferson into hiring him.

"I can fix cars, pump gas, fill tires," he pleaded. "I'm reliable and a real hard worker."

It was true, Fat thought. Hub was all those things. Give Hub anything mechanical and he'd have it taken apart and reassembled before you could turn around. It seemed to Fat that his brother had magic hands, hands that understood almost instinctively how things worked.

Bent over the engine of Grandmother Bailey's car, Mr. Jefferson continued to pick and probe and reconnect like a surgeon. He let Hub have his say. Then he shook his head. "Sorry, sonny. I got grown men with families begging me for work. I gotta turn them down, too."

He straightened up, slamming the hood shut. Fat's eyes widened as he noticed the extent of the damage to Grandmother's car. Golly. From the looks of that Ford, she and Aunt Grace were lucky to be alive.

Aunt Grace had turned pale, as though the mere sight of that car made her feel ill. She kept fiddling with her wallet in a way that made Fat figure she was worried about the cost of the repairs.

"I'm afraid she's gonna need more than a windshield and a headlight repaired," Mr. Jefferson was saying. "The generator's shot and some of the hoses have dried out pretty badly. This jalopy ain't been taken care of in a while. It's a cryin' shame." He paused, wiping his oil-stained hands and arms on a rag. "May take a coupla weeks to get the new parts in."

Grace looked dismayed. "I have to have it fixed sometime this week, Mr. Jefferson. Before Mother gets out of hospital. Or she'll have my head on a platter."

Mr. Jefferson chuckled. "That bad, eh?"

"Worse. It was all my fault. Lord knows what she'll say about the repair bill."

He could see how upset she was. "Well," he replied slowly, turning to stare at the wounded Ford. "Some of it's her own fault. This baby needs seein' to once in a while. A good checkup every so often don't cost that much." He flung his rag in a corner. " I can't make any promises. But I'll do my best, okay?"

For a second, the strain on Grace's face disappeared. "Thanks a bunch, Mr. Jefferson," she smiled. "I'd sure appreciate it."

Their way home led them past the school. Max Sutton, the physical fitness teacher, was bent over a car too. But unlike May Bailey's, this car was in pretty good shape. A dour-looking man in a black suit sat at the wheel. He was talking to Max through the open window.

Aunt Grace nudged Hub. "That's Alastair Grady, one of the school trustees," she murmured. "Get a load of that face of his. Long as a wet week."

Mr. Grady was pointing to a group of boys behind Max. They stood at some distance, waiting for Max to return and continue leading them in an outdoor exercise, an exercise Mr. Grady had evidently interrupted.

"Not much of a turn-out, eh, Sutton?" barked Mr. Grady. "The Board will be glad to hear this. We're looking for ways to cut costs."

Glancing back at the boys, Max caught sight of the Bailey trio headed home. His face broke into a smile and he gestured to them to wait.

"I'm hoping to have at least half a dozen more kids by the end of the week, Mr. Grady," he replied.

Mr. Grady gave him a cynical stare. "Bit of an optimist, eh? Times are getting tougher. Not better. You may as well know: the Board's planning on axing the school's physical education program."

Mr. Sutton didn't plead. But he wanted to, Fat could tell.

"Times are tough on kids too, Mr. Grady. Many of these kids have precious little in their lives. They need something to boost their spirits. As well as keep them fit. That's what an athletics program's all about!"

Mr. Grady flicked a finger at the gym teacher, indicating he should remove himself from the window. "English and Science is all you're gonna be teaching from now on, fella. With an appropriate cut in pay." His mouth twitched in a poor imitation of a smile. "Be seeing ya, Sutton. Principal will send you the details, formal-like. In a letter."

Max Sutton stepped back. Mr. Grady rolled up his window and drove on.

Hub and Fat both read the disappointment on Mr. Sutton's face, and they raced over to talk to him.

"Hear you got an athletics club going, Mr. Sutton," Hub said.

Mr. Sutton studied them somberly. "Sure do. Wanna join?"

"Now wait a minute, you two." Embarrassed, Grace moved in front of her nephews. "I'm sorry to have to say this to your face, Mr. Sutton. But my mother doesn't approve of you. Not since you started helping out those vagrants living down by the railway tracks."

"Vagrants? Those are men who've lost their jobs, Miss Bailey. Is that what you think, really? That anyone without a job is a vagrant?"

Grace hesitated. She was tired of having to stand behind her mother's opinions instead of voicing her own. Those men who lived down by the tracks weren't there because they wanted to be. And maybe it was better to hop a freight train and live by your wits than stay at home and watch your children go hungry. Besides, if she was in charge of the boys for awhile, maybe she should make her own decisions.

"No," she said slowly. "I guess I don't really believe that. And I think your athletic program might be just the thing for my nephews."

"Thanks, Aunt Grace!" Hub's face lit up. "I always knew you were a good egg!"

In the parched field in front of the school, the boys had given up waiting for Mr. Sutton and gone back to exercising by themselves. Mr. Sutton turned and walked over to them, followed by Fat and Hub.

"Hey, guys," he called. "Meet two new team members, Hub and Fat Bailey." He smiled at the two brothers. "Thanks," he said. "I appreciate your joining. Who knows, you might even help me hold onto my job."

The other boys crowded around the new arrivals, possibly the last members of their soon-to-be-canceled club. But Mr. Sutton was not a man to be beaten easily.

"Listen, you guys," he said suddenly. "When you go home tonight, I want you to tell all your friends, everyone you know, about the athletics club. Get as many people as you can to join. And I want you all to think real hard about how we can keep this program from being cut. Anyone has any bright ideas, I want to hear them."

Hub cleared his throat and waited, just for a moment, to see if anyone else was going to jump in.

"Mr. Sutton, sir," he blurted out at last, "I think I've got an idea!"

CHAPTER SEVEN

At first, Hub's idea floated like a lead balloon. But gradually, as he elaborated on his scheme,

Mr. Sutton became more and more excited. Finally, he clamped his hand on Hub's shoulder, wheeled him around and started marching him back into town.

"Hey, where are you going with my nephew?" demanded Grace. "We were on our way home!"

"We're gonna pitch this idea into Joe Cramp's ballpark," declared Mr. Sutton. "See what he makes of it. Why don't you come with us, Miss Bailey? Mr. Cramp likes you. We sure could use your support. You come too, Fat. You other guys get on home. We'll let you know what happens."

Grace hesitated. She should get home. There were the breakfast dishes to wash, lunch to see to. *Let them wait*, she thought daringly. *They're not important*. After all, there was no Mother at home, pointing at the clock, harping on schedules, discipline and rules. She and the boys were free. Free for a whole week!

"Sure," she said. "Of course I'll come."

Down at the *New Bedford Weekly Chronicle*, Mr. Cramp seemed to have recovered from his grammatical indigestion. He was checking over his own newspaper, sniffing idly at a cigar, when they trooped in. Tucking the cigar behind one ear, he raised his brown snap-brim hat to Grace.

"I already gave you all the envelopes we had, Miss Bailey."

Grace held up the brimming bag. "I've got plenty to be going on with, thanks, Mr. Cramp. No, the reason we're back is, um, because Mr. Sutton here has decided New Bedford should hold its own community Olympics at the fall fair picnic, you see, and ..." She let the sentence dangle, looking over pleadingly at Hub. She wanted him to talk instead of her. After all, it was his brainchild, he should be the one to explain it.

As if he'd read her mind, Hub spoke up.

"We want to invite teams from Pinebury and Golden to compete against us, Mr. Cramp."

"And why would that be, young man?" Mr. Cramp retrieved the cigar from behind his ear and gazed at it longingly.

"We want to beat the pants off them, of course." Hub grinned.

"What we're planning is a series of track and field events," Max Sutton explained, sounding more confident than he felt. "Races, high jumps, you name it, the whole shebang. But the crowning glory, the main attraction, will be the Human Pyramid."

"Just like at the circus," chimed in Hub. "Maybe we could have boxing matches, too!"

Mr. Cramp held up his cigar like a flag. "Whoa ... steady on," he protested. "This ... this Human Pyramid thing. What's that all about?"

"Well, we see that as the last and best of the competitions, the grand finale, so to speak. Each town will enter a team of ten children, one balancing on top of the other ..." Max clapped his hands together, thrusting them out and up as if in prayer. "To form a Human Pyramid, just the way it sounds."

Scowling, Mr. Cramp unwrapped his cigar. He sniffed it carefully, saying nothing.

Max lifted his chin at Grace, indicating that she should say something more. She stepped forward, racking her brains.

"You've, um ... you've always been so supportive of community events, Mr. Cramp." She smiled, pleased with herself for having hit what she considered to be just the right note. "As I'm sure you can imagine, if you sponsored the New Bedford team, this event could be a huge publicity coup for your newspaper."

Tilting back in his chair, Mr. Cramp held the cigar sideways and ran it under his nose. His scowl deepened.

Hub could stand it no longer. "Come on, Mr. Cramp," he urged. "Your community needs you.

Mr. Sutton needs you. The Board's threatening to cut his athletics program."

"We all need you," piped up Fat, inspiration suddenly dawning. "We all need what only you have: your unique flair for publicity."

Mr. Cramp's face creased into a reluctant smile. Slamming his chair onto the floor, he lit his cigar with a flourish. His shrewd brown eyes studied first Fat and then Hub as he puffed.

"So what do I have to do ..." he asked finally, through a cloud of smoke, "in return for such 'huge' publicity?"

Grace squeezed Hub's arm. Mr. Cramp had been won over. She was sure of it.

Max spoke rapidly. "You'd print up the fliers advertising the event. But what would really get the ball rolling would be if you could donate, say, a ten-dollar cash prize to the winner of the competition. Then I could ask whoever's sponsoring the teams from the other towns to chip in the same amount."

Hub and Fat held their breath as they watched Mr. Cramp turn the idea over in his mind. Ten dollars! Thirty dollars, maybe, if the other towns contributed to the prize! If their team won, some of that money would rightfully come to them! Fat could just imagine his Mom's face when they presented her with their winnings!

"What do you say, Mr. Cramp?" he blurted out. "Are you with us?"

Mr. Cramp got to his feet. He'd forgotten to blow out his match, Fat noticed. He watched as the flame crept towards the stubby, ink-stained fingers.

"What I say is ... *ouch!*"

Mr. Cramp dropped the match and stamped on it with passion.

"Did you hurt yourself?" Grace put down her bag, prepared to play Florence Nightingale.

But Mr. Cramp waved her away. "What I say is this: my New Bedford team should have team shirts. That's what I say. Team shirts with `NEW BEDFORD' emblazoned on the front. And on the back, writ large in flaming letters, the word `CHRONICLE'!" Mr. Cramp's cigar spelled the letters out in the air one by one. "That way, as the Human Pyramid takes shape, everyone will have their eyes pinned on this newspaper!"

Chomping down on his cigar and rocking back on his heels, he beamed at them.

Hub frowned. "Team shirts are expensive, Mr. Cramp. Who'd pay for them?"

Mr. Cramp chuckled. "As your patron, I guess I'll have to fork over. I wouldn't care to turn four such persuasive talkers against me! I'm assuming, of course, that New Bedford team's going to win!"

"We gotta win, sir!" said Hub, his face more serious than any twelve-year-old's ought to be.

CHAPTER EIGHT

As he walked down the street a few days later, Hub couldn't help feeling just a little pleased with himself. The Boys' Olympics was gathering momentum. The towns of Golden and Pinebury had agreed to participate in the event. With Mr. Cramp's help, posters and fliers had been printed, and the members of Mr. Sutton's athletics club had set to practicing with gusto. All that energy and goodwill, all that excitement and hope, sprang from his idea! The thought made him feel pretty darn good.

He whistled as he walked briskly past the feed store, a stack of fliers in his hand, Pal trotting at his heels. What they needed now was more boys to expand the New Bedford team. And more boys was exactly what he was determined to deliver.

"Hey, you guys! Wanna come to the Boys' Olympics?"

Outside the feed store, Gerald, Sean and

Quinn, the three Doogan brothers, loaded sacks of feed onto their father's truck. The youngest, Quinn, was in Hub's class at school, but his work-hardened air and muscular build made him seem much older. Stocky and bullnecked, with their sleepy eyes and thick speech, the brothers gave the impression of belonging to a troupe of drowsy dancing bears. Hub wondered if they could really be as slow-witted as they seemed.

The Quinns turned at his voice and stared at him blankly.

"Olympics?" queried Gerald, the eldest at six-teen. "That ain't that diner out by Pinebury, eh?"

"Well, no ... uhhh ..." Hub tried a different tack. "You fellas any good at track and field?"

"Trick and feel? What the heck's that?" asked Gerald.

"You know, running and jumping and stuff ..."

The brothers eyed each other furtively. *This fella's just plain daffy*, their look said. But politeness prevented them from saying it out loud.

Hub stuffed a flier into Sean's callused hand. "Mr. Sutton's looking for people to join his athletics club. We've challenged Pinebury and Golden to a competition on Labor Day, see? The more boys in the club, the better our chances of winning. We could win prizes ... maybe even money ..."

"'Hu-mmin Pry-a-mud ...'" Quinn read aloud over Sean's shoulder, while both Sean and Gerald listened attentively, peering at the flier. Quinn had barely struggled his way through the text when Gerald strode to the truck, jumped in the driver's seat and nodded down at Hub.

"Git in. Go on." Jerking his head at Pal. "You c'n bring yer dog."

"Why? I still got all these fliers to hand out."

"You said you need more boys, dincha? We'll find 'em for ya. Go faster in a truck than on foot. There's the Humphreys out by the Lower Road— they got two boys. And the Naughtons, down Pilton Lane way—they got six. Ain't easy to walk there. Git in."

It was what his dad had always said: you can't judge a book by its cover. As Hub, squeezed in between sacks of feed, crisscrossed the county with the Doogan boys, he learned that the only thing slow about them was their speech. Sure, their knowledge of the world was limited. During peak laboring seasons on the farm, they barely made it to school. But they had an innate intelligence and a warmth of heart that helped Hub feel at ease with them.

The Doogans knew every single family with

boys in the area, knew how to get there and how to make themselves heard when they arrived. They knew about animals, too. No farm dog threatened to bite or even growl at the boys as they made their rounds.

It was Gerald who proved to Hub just how smart a dog Pal was. Hub had jumped out of the truck to stuff a flier in the Thompsons' mailbox, which stood at the top of a long country lane.

"Here, give it to me," Gerald said, taking the flier from Hub and handing it to Pal. Then he snapped his fingers. "C'mon, me beauty. Mail the letter now, there's a good boy."

Pal's ears twitched. Bounding to the mailbox he opened the flap and nuzzled the flier inside, letting the lid snap shut before pushing the flag down with his nose.

Hub watched in disbelief.

"Them country dogs is a whole lot smarter than you think," grinned Gerald, sauntering back to the truck. He didn't say: "So are the people." He didn't need to.

Next day, surrounded by a bevy of eager boys, Max Sutton looked over at Hub and smiled his thanks. Again, Hub felt a surge of pride.

"This is one heck of an improved turn-out,

Hub!" Max shouted over the din of noisy, aspiring athletes.

Hub slapped Quinn on the back. "I couldn't have done it without the Doogans, Mr. Sutton," he yelled back.

Max blew his whistle hard. "All right. Now it's down to work, fellas. We've got a whole lot of practicing to do. It's gonna be worth our while, too. Pinebury and Golden have each agreed to raise the Grand Prize money to twenty dollars!"

Twenty dollars! Hub and Fat exchanged glances. If each of the three towns threw in twenty dollars, that made the prize money soar to sixty! Sixty dollars!

"Now all we gotta do is win the Grand Prize, huh Fat?" whispered Hub.

"Just think of Mom's face when we hand it over!" replied Fat, his eyes shining.

For the next couple of days every single boy on the team poured his energy into practicing. They did push-ups and jumping jacks. They ran single file. They ran in place. They somersaulted and cartwheeled. They stood in rows and touched their palms to their feet till they thought their heads would burst. And when they felt like dropping with exhaustion they ran some more. They jumped over small hurdles and large hurdles. They lifted

weights. They practiced discus and javelin throwing. They formed pairs and honed their three-
legged racing skills. For the wheelbarrow race they
formed partners again: one boy scurried on his
hands to the finish line, his legs held like handles
by his partner. They ran the egg-and-spoon race.
They practiced dropping to their hands and knees
while other boys climbed on top of them and more
boys knelt on the top layer, before collapsing in a
heap, the Human Pyramid reduced to a tangle of
bruised legs and laughing kids.

Hub couldn't believe how well things were
going, how much fun they were having. He forgot
how worried he'd been. He could almost feel the
prize money in his hands.

And then, quite literally, the bottom fell out of
his pyramid of dreams.

CHAPTER NINE

It happened one morning while Hub was leading a
small group in jumping jacks. Another bunch of
boys was fine-tuning the assembly of the first two
layers of the pyramid.

A truck skidded onto the brown grass of the

playing field. At first Hub paid no attention. Then he heard Sean Doogan give an outraged bellow. Glancing over, Hub saw a bear of a man in grubby overalls lifting Sean and Quinn by the scruff of the neck and carting them off towards the truck.

"Take yer mitts offa me, Pa!" Sean was hollering. "I'm only practicing me discus!"

"I'll practice me fistus on yeez all if ye don't get home this minute," fumed their father, hurling his sons at the truck. "I'll tan the hides offa yeez, so I will. Haven't I got fields beggin' to be hayed, while yeez are prancin' about like fairies?"

"Hey Pa! Put 'em down!" Gerald was only slightly smaller than his father but every bit as muscular.

"You too, get in that truck. Now!" his father roared, swiping at the young man's head. Swallowing his anger, Gerald followed his brothers. He knew better than to tempt his father's wrath.

Hub couldn't believe his eyes. The Doogans, his Doogans, were leaving!

Max Sutton approached the burly farmer. "Can I help you, Mr. Doogan?"

"Some help you are!" Turning, Doogan pushed his sweat-stained hat back on his head and spat at the ground by the teacher's feet.

"What exactly is the problem?" asked Max quietly.

Doogan's face was mottled with anger. "You! You're the problem, so you are. I'm trying to get my haying done and you've got my boys here playing hop, skip and jump!"

Apart from the spring sowing, harvest time was the most crucial event in a farmer's year. His whole livelihood depended on it. Even if he'd wanted to, Max knew better than to interfere.

"I'm sorry," he said. "I didn't realize you had haying to be done."

Doogan glared around, breathing heavily. Any minute now he might start pawing the ground and snorting, Hub thought, smoke billowing from his nostrils. Over Max's shoulder the farmer noticed the boys constructing their pyramid. The sight seemed to calm him.

"I've lost two days' work thanks to you," he snapped at Max. Perhaps it was by way of an explanation, because he instantly addressed the pyramid-builders. "Anybody else wanna work?" he barked. "I'm paying fifty cents a day."

"Let's go!" Without hesitation, the boys tumbled to the ground and raced to join the three captive Doogan brothers.

Hub's heart sank.

Max blew his whistle. "Hey, wait! Just four!" he yelled. "The rest of you get back to your practicing." With whoops of triumph, the first four boys hurled themselves onto the truck. In the midst of hard times, no one in his right mind could refuse fifty cents a day!

"Will you let 'em back when they finish the haying? " Max asked.

"Don't count on it," growled Doogan. Slamming himself into the driver's seat, he roared off.

Hub watched his hopes disappear in a cloud of dust.

"That's the whole base of our pyramid right there, driving off in that truck!" he protested. "What're we gonna do, Mr. Sutton? We need at least two more guys to hold us all up."

Max scratched his head. "I dunno. I think we've just about used up all the boys in town, Hub."

Hub's throat constricted. *This can't be happening*, he thought to himself.

But it was. Like everything else bad that had befallen him, it had happened suddenly. Out of the blue. He felt like giving up, right then and there. But then he thought about his mother: after all that had happened, she must feel like giving up too. But she hadn't. She'd kept on, struggling to present an appearance of courage to the world.

He would do that too, he decided abruptly. It was the least he could do for her. He'd fight for that prize money, dammit, if it took every ounce of strength he had.

He looked up. Mr. Sutton was watching him. His eyes were sad.

"Gimme some more fliers, Mr. Sutton," Hub said. "There's still one place in town I haven't tried."

Hub didn't tell Fat where he was going. He sneaked off after lunch, when Fat and Aunt Grace were listening to "The Craigs," one of their favorite serials on the radio.

Now, as he pushed open the door and stepped inside the pool hall, he was glad he hadn't taken his little brother along. Thin slivers of sun sliced their way through stained slat blinds, weakly illuminating clouds of tobacco smoke. In the long, shadowed room, the air hung thick and spiritless, like the men slumped at the counter. The place reeked of unwashed bodies, stale beer and hopelessness.

Hub stood by the door for a moment, letting his eyes adjust to the murk. It was as if he'd slipped from the glare of the street right down a rabbit hole into a forgotten, timeless world. He felt out of place and impossibly young. *Think of the prize money,* he told himself. *Think of Mom.*

Over by one of the pool tables, two skinny guys were arguing over a dog-eared magazine. They wore soiled undershirts, their hair greased back. One of them had a tattoo on his upper arm. Hub couldn't tell how old they were. Maybe they were men already. Maybe they'd yell at him, or worse, poke fun at him. He swallowed hard and moved towards them.

"Say, would you guys know anyone who might be interested in ... in track ...? You know ... sports?"

The one with the tattoo had a faint mustache crowning his upper lip, a fedora slung low over his brow. His eyes flicked over Hub like a razor, sharp with contempt. "I know track," he said. "You know track, Buck?" He had a high-pitched, nasal voice.

Buck was smaller. Hub could tell he was in awe of his companion. "Sure, I know track, Tony," he replied. "As in 'makin' tracks,' eh?"

Tony scratched his tattoo lazily. Draped over his right biceps, a buxom mermaid held a huge lobster to her ear. His eyes traveled once again over Hub. "How 'bout I help you make tracks back outside, kid?" he drawled. "I think one swift kick in the butt should do it."

Buck guffawed. Tony tossed the magazine at his fawning friend and advanced on Hub.

Hub grinned and held out his fliers. Okay, so these guys were older than he was. But not by much. He'd stopped feeling scared. Up close, he could see what they were. They were boys trying to look like men. Men they thought were tough. What they were was frightened. Now he knew how to talk to them.

"Look," he said. "Sixty bucks. We got sixty bucks riding on this Human Pyramid thing, right here." He let the sixty bucks sink in for a second as he handed them each a flier. Then he added, "We need more athletes. Tough guys, know what I mean?"

As he expected, the money stopped Tony dead.

"Sixty bucks?" he repeated.

"Split by the winning team," Hub interjected quickly. He reached to take back the fliers. "Only I guess you guys ain't interested."

"Hey!" Tony snatched his flier, raising it over Hub's head. "Who says we ain't interested? For sixty smackers, jeez, I'd clean toilets in hell."

"You'd have to join Mr. Sutton's athletics club. He's our gym teacher at school."

For the first time, Tony looked abashed. "Darn," he said. "I ain't allowed on school property. I got expelled, see?"

Buck swelled with reflected pride. "Meet Tony Piretti, kid. He's the guy set fire to Mr. Grady's shed. Guess you know who Mr. Grady is, eh? One of them guys on the school board."

Mr. Grady? The name sounded familiar to Hub but he couldn't quite place it.

"This isn't a school matter," he said, "least I don't think it is. This is a club, see? An athletics club."

Tony's eyes were glued to the flier. "Sixty bucks!" he muttered longingly, broken finger-nails drumming on his tattoo. "Okay," he said finally, looking straight at Hub. "You got your-self a deal."

Hub tried not to whoop in triumph. He kept his face serious. "You'll need a clean shirt, both of you. And you'd better keep your sleeves rolled down," he said to Tony. "Mr. Sutton don't like mermaids."

"Anything else, Mother Superior?" drawled Tony. But there was a glint of humor in his eyes.

"Yeah." Now Hub couldn't keep the grin off his face. "No slouchin', no swearin' and, above all, no grinnin'. Anyone found havin' fun will be dragged off the premises and shot at dawn."

Buck turned quickly to Tony, checking his response. Had this weird kid just made a threat? Or a joke? When he saw Tony grinning, Buck laughed loudly.

It took Tony and Buck more than an hour to get washed and unearth clean shirts. Hub waited for them on a bench outside the feed store. The smoke from the pool hall had made his stomach queasy and he was glad to have the chance to sit in the sun and breathe in clean air.

He hardly recognized Buck and Tony when they returned. Although pale, they both seemed more energetic, brighter. He noted with surprise that Tony was a good-looking kid.

As they walked together onto the playing field, Hub saw Mr. Sutton raise his hands to his eyes against the sun's glare and study the three of them.

"I got two more, Mr. Sutton," he said simply.

Buck took over the introductions. "This is my friend Tony Piretti, Mr. Sutton," he said smoothly. "And I'm Buck Mayhew. We're here for the Human Pyram—"

"You're darn tootin' we are!" Tony interrupted. Hub could see he was nervous. "We heard about that sixty bucks. And we're gonna make damn sure we win it."

"Good to meet you both," Max Sutton said, shaking their hands. He led them off to meet the other members of the club.

Later that afternoon, Max took Hub aside.

"I've heard of Tony Piretti somewhere," he said. "Something tells me both have a bad reputation."

"Just give 'em a chance, Mr. Sutton," urged Hub. "They're pretty keen, 'specially Tony. Besides, we need 'em real bad if we wanna win the competition."

Max nodded. "I know how hard you tried on this one, Hub. Don't think I don't appreciate it." He raised a warning finger. "But ... with hooligans like that on the team, we'd better win. Or we're in serious trouble."

Hub tried to laugh it off. "Piece of cake, sir!" he grinned. But he felt uneasy. He'd made himself responsible for these guys now.

What if something went wrong?

CHAPTER TEN

"Twenty-five dollars?" Grace tried to keep the note of dismay out of her voice. She blinked up at Mr. Jefferson.

"That's right, Miss Bailey." Standing in the doorway of the Bailey mansion, Jefferson went through the items on his bill again. "You did ask us to get it done fast, remember, Miss? Before your Ma came home? I had to put my best man on it, working overtime. Them's his hours, right there. See?"

Grace nodded, unseeing. The figures danced before her eyes, turning into exclamation points of panic.

Mr. Jefferson handed over the bill. "I'd, uh ... I'd sure be grateful if you could settle this up soon as possible, Miss."

Wouldn't that be nice? If she could just march straight to her purse and hand over the money, just like that? If she had her own money. Real money, not just the pin money the New Jersey stamp company paid her. If she didn't have to go begging to her mother for almost every penny.

"Can you wait till tomorrow?" she asked, realizing the man was expecting an answer. "I'll ... I'll have to get the money from my mother in the hospital."

Mr. Jefferson touched his cap. "That'll be fine, Miss Bailey." He turned and walked down the front steps.

Grace glanced at the car standing in the roadway. He must have washed it, too. Behind the white picket fence it gleamed, sleek and powerful. Like a threat. She dreaded ever having to go near it again.

"Mr. Jefferson," she called. "Could I trouble

you to pull the car into the driveway for me? I ...
um ..." She gave a nervous giggle. "I don't really
feel like touching it."

His face betrayed his surprise. "Why sure," he
responded politely. "I'd be happy too."

How could anyone, he wondered, not feel up
to driving such a dandy machine?

Grace took Hub and Fat with her to the hospital.
More and more, she had noticed, her mother
seemed to depend on their company, even enjoy it.

"What's this?" Mrs. Bailey mumbled as Grace
nervously handed over Mr. Jefferson's bill. *Please,
Lord*, she prayed. *Don't let there be an argument. Not
now. Not right here in the hospital.*

Bruises, purple and black, stretched down the
right side of her mother's face. The lid of her right
eye refused to open properly. It hung, discolored
and puffy, like a theatre curtain. Holding the bill
close to her left eye, May peered at it in silence.
Grace stood behind the boys waiting for the explo-
sion. She didn't have long to wait.

"Twenty-five dollars! That's sheer extortion!"
For someone who looked so ill, May Bailey's voice
sounded remarkably strong. She dragged herself
upright on the pillows.

"It wasn't just the accident, Mother. A whole

lot of work needed to be done. Mr. Jefferson said we'd been neglecting —"

"That's the last time I'm letting you near that car again. Now hand me that purse."

Grace didn't know whether to laugh or cry. She'd hoped her mother would react that way, would once again forbid her to learn to drive. And yet ... more than anything else in her life, that car represented freedom. Her ticket to a life of her own.

Fat dug his grandmother's purse out from under a blanket and handed it over. Carefully, she counted out twenty-five dollars.

"I don't know what came over me," she grumbled, handing the money to her daughter. "Letting you learn to drive, just like that. I should have my head examined."

You did, Grace wanted to snap, *and all they found was sawdust*. But she restrained herself. It was beginning to look as if the concussion had made her mother completely forget her strategy for saving Grace from the attentions of a particular traveling salesman. "It's much more sensible for me to take the boys to see Honey on the bus, the way I used to,"she said brightly, wondering if her mother could really have forgotten all about Judd Wainwright.

But memory stirred in May Bailey. There was

something she'd forgotten. What was it? Something to do with a bus ... with Grace traveling on the bus and some sort of bad influence ...? Oh dear, it was slipping from her grasp again. All that was left was the certainty that, as far as Grace was concerned, buses were out of bounds.

"Certainly not," she said, striving to reassert her authority, to give no hint of her loss of memory. "From now on ..." She had to come up with a new plan, in a hurry. "From now on ... Robert will drive the boys to see their mother. Once a month." There, she'd managed that pretty well!

"Once a month!" Hub and Fat protested simultaneously. And May knew immediately that she'd made a mess of something, whatever it was. They were yelping and mewling, both of them.

"You said we could see her once every two weeks. You *promised*!"

"I'm tired," she said abruptly. "No more applesauce from either of you, you hear me? Or you won't be going anywhere ever again. Now find my book for me, Henry. I want to be read to."

Fat sighed. Normally he enjoyed reading aloud. But he was so mad at his grandmother he felt like hurling a whole library of books at her head. Only see Mom once a month! How could a grandmother be so cruel?

Dr. Barlow opened the door just then. "May I see you for a minute, Miss Bailey?" he asked pleasantly.

Grace stepped out into the corridor, leaving the door partly ajar. Fat picked up the book from the table by his grandmother's bed. It was one he'd never seen before. "'A Tale of Two Cities,'" he read aloud. "'By Charles Dickens. Book the First—Recalled to Life.'" He glanced at his grandmother. She was gazing fretfully out the door at her daughter in conference with the doctor. Fat cleared his throat. Raising his voice slightly, he began. "'Chapter One. It was the best of times. It was the worst of times ...'"

With a small sigh of pleasure, May relaxed against the pillows. She closed her eyes, shutting out everything but the words.

Standing in the corridor, Grace felt her dark mood lighten as she listened to Dr. Barlow.

"We'd like your mother to consider staying with us a week longer," he was saying. "We need to do further tests. It's that right eye of hers we're concerned about. "

Grace felt a pang of shame. Here she was, thrilled silly because her mother might have to extend her hospital stay. Without a single thought for the health of the woman who'd brought her into this world. "How serious is it, Doctor?" she asked remorsefully.

"We're not sure. Without the right treatment, without proper care and rest, she could lose all sight in that eye."

"I guess she won't get too much rest at home, Doctor. Those boys are far too energetic."

Dr. Barlow studied her in silence. Then he smiled. "I'll speak to your mother myself," he said. "You get on home now, with the boys." He stepped into the room.

Grace leaned wearily against the wall. What she had said was true. The boys *were* energetic. They *would* tire her mother. But all the same, she felt like a hypocrite. Because the emotion that flooded over her was not genuine concern for her mother's health, but relief.

Another week of freedom! Another chance to try to see Judd without Mother getting in the way!

CHAPTER ELEVEN

Honey shifted the earpiece to her other ear. Why didn't someone answer? Where was everyone? Glancing at her watch she saw that her five minutes

were up. She'd better get back or her boss, Mr.
Molloy, would have something to say. She let the
phone ring three more times, then hung up.

Standing in the cramped office off the storeroom, she straightened her back and adjusted her
apron. The children were an ache that never left her.
When she was tired and hungry, as she was now,
the ache grew unbearable. Sometimes she thought
she wasn't going to be able to cope, she missed
them so much. She remembered reading somewhere about soldiers wounded during the First
World War. Long after their legs or arms had been
amputated, they continued to feel pain in the missing limbs. That was how she felt. Her kids had
become her phantom limbs.

Leaving the storeroom, she hurried back to
work. Evening was drawing in. She hoped Mr.
Molloy would have left by now. But no, she could
hear his voice coming from the shop. It was low,
almost confidential. By the doorway she paused,
fearful of interrupting something important.

"If you could start Monday," she heard her
boss say. "That would be an opportune time."

A woman was standing by the till, a bag of groceries held at her hip. She had her back to Honey.
"Thank you, Mr. Molloy," she said. "I sure do
appreciate it."

Why, that's Lucille! Honey thought. *Why didn't she come say hello to me the way she normally does?* Lucille Twomey lived a few blocks down the street from Honey. She had a daugher only a few months younger than Violet. Usually, when she was shopping at Mr. Molloy's grocery, Lucille would exchange a few words with Honey as she swept the floor or restocked the shelves. Honey always made sure she had some small treat in her apron pocket for Lucille's little girl.

"We open the store at eight," Mr. Molloy was saying. "So if you could be here at seven-thirty, that'd give you plenty of time to make sure everything's in order."

Surely he wasn't taking on another worker, Honey thought. He'd done nothing but complain about costs since she started! It took a moment for what she had heard to sink in. She stepped into the store, trying to ward off the sudden panic inside her.

At the counter, Lucille and Mr. Molloy had stopped talking and turned to look at her. Lucille wrapped both arms around her groceries and nodded at Mr. Molloy.

"I'll see you on Monday, Mr. Molloy," she said.

She had to pass Honey on her way out.

"Where's the fire, Lucille?" Honey willed

Lucille to look her in the eye. "Don't I even get a hello any more?"

Lucille kept going. "Sorry, Honey," she mumbled. "Gotta run. I left the baby with my mother." Her gaze fluttered in the direction of Honey's face, coming to rest near her chin.

Mr. Molloy busied himself at the till. "Your break lasted longer than five minutes, Mrs. Bailey. Not for the first time."

He couldn't look her in the eye either, Honey saw. "I'm sorry, Mr. Molloy," she said, trying to keep her voice steady. "I couldn't get through to the exchange. It was busy. Then when I finally got connected to New Bedford, there was no answer."

He wasn't listening. He had taken the day's cash from the till and was counting it. "Lucille Twomey came to see me last week," he said, keeping his eyes on the money. "She offered to take your job for three dollars a week, instead of the five I'm paying you. She has as much experience as you have, Mrs. Bailey. More, if the truth be told." He glanced at her, steeling himself. "I've told her she can have the job."

Honey rested her hands on the counter to stop them shaking. Taking several dollars from the small pile he had counted out, the grocer stuffed them into an envelope. "This is what I owe you for the week, Mrs. Bailey. You may leave now. I'll close up the store myself tonight."

"Please, Mr. Molloy! I've got kids to support. I need the money, truly I do." She couldn't keep her voice from trembling.

"We all have kids to support," Mr. Molloy said, closing the drawer of the till. "I have to do what's best for business."

"What if I agreed to take less, to go as low as Lucille?"

"No. It's all arranged now. She starts Monday. I gave her my word."

Yeah, but only a few weeks ago it was me you gave your word too, Honey wanted to retort. But she knew it was hopeless. Taking off her apron, she picked up the envelope and walked out of the store.

The ache was really bad now. *Hub, Fat, Violet.* She repeated her children's names like a mantra as she walked blindly down the street towards the apartment she had once shared with her brother, the apartment she now had to pay for by herself. She didn't dare say *Jack.* If she said her husband's name, the tears would start for sure. *Hub, Fat, Violet. My sons. My baby daughter.* She had to see them soon. She had to. At least Hub and Fat could make the trip to come visit. She would try calling

Grace again from the rooming house, arrange for her to bring them up this weekend.

Climbing the stairs, she realized she was starving. She'd forgotten to get anything to eat. An envelope stuck out from under her door. Bending down to retrieve it, she saw it was a notice from North Bridge Savings and Loan, reminding her of the rent increase due next week.

She didn't make it inside. Right there, in the darkened corridor, with the smell of Mr. Mitchell's stewed cabbage rising from the first floor, she broke down. Crouching by the locked door she wept for everything she had lost. For Jack, her beloved Jack. For Violet, her lost daughter. For Hub and Fat, her missing boys. She wept because she'd been fired, because now she wouldn't have enough money to pay the rent, and because she'd absolutely no idea what she was going to do next.

CHAPTER TWELVE

Fat's nose had been out of joint for some time now. Everyone else seemed to be better at sports than he was. Take Hub, for instance. In one day of practice drills alone, Hub had scored first in the high jump and second in the javelin and discus throw. One or another of the Doogan brothers had come first in the three-legged race, the wheelbarrow race and the long-distance run. No one else in the entire group had done conspicuously badly. Except Fat. The only race he hadn't come last in had been the egg-and-spoon. Bad enough being called Fat, he thought morosely. At least he was used to that. But darn it, being a loser in sports was enough to make a guy quit getting out of bed in the morning.

"You're the youngest in the whole group," Hub kept telling him. "Just keep practicing and you'll find something you're good at. Once you've found it, then you gotta concentrate on doing it hard as you can."

Yeah. Sure. Easy for him to say.

And then one day, when the group was working on the pyramid for the umpteenth time, Fat found that being the youngest and the smallest paid off.

He'd been kneeling on Tony Piretti's shoulders when suddenly Tony bent down and shook him off.

"Hey, watch it!" Fat yelled as his butt hit the grass with a thwack. But Tony ignored him, calling out to Mr. Sutton, "Hey, coach! This pyramid ain't working. You know why? Cause the whole goldarn balance is way off, that's why."

"Go on," said Mr. Sutton. "I'm listening."

"Take a look at Archie here," commanded Tony. Archie Morris, who took the position at the peak of the pyramid, had spiraled down from the top when Fat had fallen and now lay spread-eagled on the grass. "He's a whole head taller and maybe two pounds fatter than Fat."

"Fatter than Fat," Buck Mayhew sniggered. "Sounds like a riddle: What's two heads taller and fatter than Fat?"

Mr. Sutton ignored him. He was looking at Tony. "So?"

"So Archie don't belong on top," concluded Tony. He pointed at Fat. "Fat belongs on top."

"Yeah," snorted Buck. "Cause Fat always rises to the top!"

Mr. Sutton sized Fat up. "Tony's right," he said. "Give it a whirl, Fat."

So the guys had reassembled, grumbling all the while. Fat clambered up over Tony, taking special care to yank, accidentally on purpose, Buck's greasy hair. Then he hauled himself up over the Naughton boys, and, doing his best not to wobble, he slowly knelt upright.

Mr. Sutton stood back. "That's it! A perfect pyramid. You're our ace, Fat."

Fat forced himself to look down. The formation

held. Not a wobble in sight. Raising his arms high, he gave a whoop of elation.

"Nerves of steel!" Mr. Sutton smiled up at him. "That's what the guy on top needs: nerves of steel and a cool head."

It was Mr. Sutton who needed nerves of steel a few days later, when the school principal walked into the gym accompanied by a grim-looking man carrying a clipboard, a pencil stuck behind one ear.

"This gentleman's here to appraise the school's sports equipment," Mr. Pagnutti said to Mr. Sutton. "He's an auctioneer." His words caused a hush to fall amongst the boys. Suddenly the threat to their athletics program had become a reality.

"Appraise the sports equipment?" Mr. Sutton looked stricken.

Mr. Pagnutti stepped closer. "So that he can auction it off. Get rid of it." His diction was clipped and precise, Fat noticed, as though Mr. Sutton were a very young student.

Someone yanked Fat from behind, pulling him over to stand closer to Hub. It was Tony Piretti.

"Cover me up! Quick!" Tony whispered. "Pagnutti said he'd have me arrested if he caught me on school property again!" Buck cowered beside him. Fat grabbed Archie and the three of them stood tall, forming a human wall to hide Tony. It might have worked, too, except that Buck lost his balance and fell over on top of Archie, who stumbled forward yelling as though he'd been shot.

What a jerk! thought Fat in disgust. *Screeching like a stuck pig! Why can't he just fall quietly?*

Of course, once the human wall was breached, Mr. Pagnutti's eagle eye detected Tony easily.

"May I ask what that hoodlum's doing on school property?" he demanded of Mr. Sutton.

Mr. Sutton sighed. Fat could see his tolerance was wearing thin. "Look, Mr. Pagnutti," he replied, keeping his voice low. "An athletics program is just what a kid like Tony needs. It'll help build his self-confidence."

His words were wasted on Pagnutti. "Don't give me that bleeding-heart stuff, Sutton! I had that bum expelled!" he thundered. "What the hell d'you think Alastair Grady's gonna say if he finds out the reprobate who burned down his shed is still tolerated around this school? Now get rid of him!"

"He needs a second chance, Mr. Pagnutti."

The principal's jaw clenched. He stepped right up to Max Sutton. Mr. Pagnutti was a big man, bigger than the gym teacher. His very proximity was threatening.

"I said get rid of him! I want him out of here before Grady finds out and closes down the entire Olympic event. Do you understand me?"

Max said nothing.

"These old desks over here, Mr. Pagnutti!" the auctioneer hollered, breaking the silence. "Did you want them listed too?"

Mr. Pagnutti turned on his heel and marched over to join the auctioneer.

Max blew his whistle. "Okay, guys. Everyone outside. Let's go."

Fat didn't want to go. He wanted to make sure Mr. Sutton was all right. He hung around at the back of the classroom when the others left. In the far corner, Mr. Pagnutti conversed with the auctioneer, but he was watching Mr. Sutton too, Fat noticed.

"Hey, Piretti!" the gym teacher called to Tony. On his way out the door, Tony paused and came back. There was a look of dread on his face.

"Yeah, Coach?"

Mr. Sutton stepped back slightly, so that he was out of earshot of Pagnutti. "I've been watching you, Piretti," he began.

Fat couldn't help feeling disappointed. Was Mr. Sutton really going to fire Tony? If it hadn't been for Piretti, Fat might never have made it to the top of the pyramid.

"I can see you've been trying really hard. I just want to tell you, you're doing fine. Keep up the good work, okay?"

Tony's face was a study in surprise and confusion. The same way Fat felt.

"Now get out there and have some fun," Sutton concluded.

The hurt in Tony's eyes vanished behind a grin. "Thanks, Coach," was all he said.

Mr. Sutton was grinning too when he turned round and caught sight of Fat. "I thought I said everyone out!" he said.

"I'm going! I'm going!"

But as Fat ran onto the playing field, he couldn't help wondering what would happen when the Boys' Olympics took place. Both Mr. Pagnutti and Mr. Grady were bound to be there. What would happen when they clapped eyes on Tony Piretti?

CHAPTER THIRTEEN

Over dinner, while Hub was telling Aunt Grace all about the auctioneer in the gymnasium, the phone rang. Fat got to it first. From the way his younger brother's eyes lit up, Hub knew it was Mom on the line. He got up from the table and went to stand beside Fat, waiting his turn.

Fat was blabbing about the Boys' Olympics. On and on he prattled about the Human Pyramid and Archie Morris and what a great guy Tony Piretti was. He described Buck Mayhew as "that pimply, big-mouth, mooncalf, buck-toothed hooligan" and bragged about how he, Fat, had been picked to climb to the top of the pyramid. Hub shifted from foot to foot, his impatience mounting.

"Our team's gonna win the Grand Prize in the competition, Mom," Fat chattered. Hub felt like throttling him. That bit was supposed to be a secret. He didn't want Mom knowing anything about the prize money until they were ready to place it in her hands. He grabbed the receiver before Fat had a chance to mention "money."

"Hi, Mom."

He tried to picture her, standing there in the badly lit corridor outside her apartment, where the public phone hung. He remembered how little strips of wallpaper had been torn off the wall around the phone—probably so people could write telephone numbers on them. There were numbers scrawled on the wall, too. And rude words. When she'd first moved in with Uncle Joe,

Mom had sworn she was going to clean that wall, maybe even put new wallpaper up. She'd worn red patches on her knees washing the floor in the corridor, scrubbing the filthy linoleum until it shone. "The Queen of Clean," that's what she called herself. Show those germs no mercy. The telephone wall, she declared, would be her next victim. But then Uncle Joe had skedaddled, taking what was left of Mom's money. After that, she'd been too busy trying to make ends meet to clean floors, let alone tackle walls.

"You guys coming to see me this weekend?" Her voice sounded different, muffled somehow.

"We can't, Mom. Mr. Sutton's counting on us for the competition, you know, the Boys' Olympics Fat was telling you about? It's being held Saturday. We really have to be here. So ... Mom?"

She was silent for a minute. Then she said brightly, "Boy, that club of yours sure sounds like a whole lot of fun. I wish I could be there to see my boys hopping around in sacks and turning themselves into pyramids ... "

The muffled sound was worse. Her voice trailed off. He thought maybe she'd let the earpiece fall.

"Have you got a cold, Mom?" That must be what was wrong. He could hear her blowing her nose. Another long silence. "Mom?" he repeated, raising his voice.

She was back on the line. She cleared her throat. Her voice was still husky. "Let me speak to Grace, sweetie, okay?"

Hub stood to one side so Aunt Grace could talk. A worry, small as a toad, crawled into his belly. He tried pretending it wasn't there.

"How are you, Honey?"

The smile on Aunt Grace's face faded as she listened to whatever his mother was saying.

"Well, yes, the car's all fixed now. Uh-huh. Mr. Jefferson brought it back the other day. Along with a big fat bill ... What? Oh Honey ..." Her voice climbed the scale. "I couldn't. Really I couldn't. For one thing, Mother's absolutely forbidden me to touch her car. And for another, the thought of driving it gives me the willies. I mean, I've only had *one* driving lesson, for God's sake, and that ended in disaster ... What?"

Hub wanted to grab the earpiece from Aunt Grace. He had to put his hands firmly in his pockets to stop himself. The toad in his stomach started to jump around.

"I know the two weeks are up, Honey," Grace was saying. Her voice had gone all calm and soothing. "Yes, I know you're due a visit from them. But for some reason Mother's gotten it in her head that the boys can only go see you once a month now ... Honey? Are you okay? No, it's true, I'm afraid. I'm not allowed to bring them any more. No, honestly. That's what she said. From now on it's Bob who's gonna bring them. Once a month. I'm really, really sorry. Honey? Honey, what's wrong?"

Aunt Grace was still for a long moment, listening. Once or twice her eyes flickered over to where Hub and Fat stood, rigid with attention. Then she cocked her head towards the earpiece, as though in disbelief. She sighed and hung up.

"I wasn't finished talking to her," Fat protested.

"What's wrong?" Hub asked quickly. "Did she tell you what's wrong?"

Grace blinked at him, her eyes full of concern. "She hung up on me."

Hub felt sick with worry. "Something's wrong," he said slowly. "She's in trouble of some kind. I can just tell. We gotta go see her."

His little brother moved closer. "You think she needs us, Hub?"

"Now just a minute." Aunt Grace sat down heavily on one of the kitchen chairs. Their unfinished meal lay cold on the table. She tried to think of something comforting to say. In her head she could still hear what Honey had said before she hung up: "Nothing's wrong. Nothing!" But she was sobbing. "Don't say anything to the boys. I don't want to upset them. Just tell them I ... I ... understand. I'll see you all real soon."

Grace frowned, idly pushing the lumps of food around on her plate with her fork. Honey was usually such a sunny person. Despite everything that had happened to her, she always seemed to find the inner strength to fight back. Something must have gone badly wrong for her to break down on the phone like that. Still, she had asked Grace not to upset the boys, and she would try to respect that request. She jumped to her feet and began clearing the table. "I'm sure it's nothing serious." She used her brisk voice. "She's probably just feeling a tiny bit lonely, that's all."

Her nephews stared back at her solemnly. Hub had slung his arm around Fat. She liked that about them, she thought, as she piled the dirty plates one on top of the other. The way they always stood together when things got rough. They were loyal kids. Loyal to each other and to their mother.

"Look," she said now, trying to cheer them up. "Let's just stack the dishes. They'll keep till morning. You guys go get ready for bed, while I make some cocoa. We'll drink it listening to the radio, okay? And no more worrying about your mom. As I said, she's probably just lonely."

Hub looked white as a sheet. She hoped he wasn't getting sick.

Fat spoke up. "If she was so lonely, why'd she hang up?" he asked.

CHAPTER FOURTEEN

That night, Grace dreamt about Judd Wainwright. She was driving her mother's car along a country lane, when suddenly, far in the distance, she became aware of a small, bulky figure walking by the side of the road. His back was to her, but she knew it was Judd. Slamming her foot into the accelerator, she urged the car forward. But instead of speeding up, its pace slackened and dropped off. The engine coughed, choked, died. She pressed the starter button, twice, three times. She hammered on the horn. Silence.

"Judd!" she screamed. "Wait! Wait for me!"

But the shadow marched on, seeming not to hear.

She awoke with a start, drenched in sweat. Heart pounding, she lay for a moment trying to figure out where she was. There was no car. There was no Judd. Through the long window in her bedroom the early morning sun flooded in. But wait, that *was* a car she was hearing. That wasn't a dream. It sounded like a car refusing to start, the engine wheezing and stalling. It sounded like Mother's car, as a matter of fact.

"Good Lord!" Grace jumped from her bed, grabbed her dressing gown and ran to the window.

Down below, her mother's pride and joy was creeping down the driveway. She peered down, puzzled. Maybe she should call the police. But surely no thief would drive at such a snail's pace!

Just then, Pal stuck his doggy head out the back window of the car, and Fat's arm, followed by his head, appeared from the front passenger side, stroking Pal's ears. For Pete's sake! It was the boys! The boys were stealing Mother's car! Dear Lord, the boys were driving!

With a shriek, Grace raced down the stairs and out the front door.

"No! Wait! You can't do this! Please, boys. What if you have an accident? Think about your-selves. Think about the car!"

The Ford lurched forward. It was about to turn onto the street when the motor stalled.

"Hubert!" Grace called sternly as she ran over,

clutching her dressing gown to her. "Have you lost your senses?"

Hub sat in the driver's seat, staring straight ahead. "Our mother's in trouble, Aunt Grace. We've got to help her."

Grace pressed closer to the window. "Didn't you promise you'd never run away again?"

"We don't need your permission," Fat told her, a defiant look in his brown eyes. "We can run away again any time we need to."

Hub pressed the starter button again.

Grace put her hand on the car, as if to detain it. She could tell by her nephews' expressions she had no choice. She would have to do the very thing she dreaded.

"All right," she said, giving in. "I will drive you, if that will stop you driving yourselves. But you have to come back exactly when I say. We simply cannot miss Mother's visiting hours tomorrow." She groaned as the full extent of what she was about to do hit her. "If Mother ever found out that I'd taken the car, against her express orders, my God, she'd have my guts for garters!"

"She won't find out," Hub reassured her. "We have to be back for the competition tomorrow afternoon, too. It's just ... we gotta see Mom, find out what's wrong."

"We *want* to be back here on time, Aunt Grace. We've gotta win that prize money for Mom, see?"

Looking at their worried faces, Grace felt a sudden pang of jealousy. Sure, Honey had her troubles. But these two boys made up for an awful lot. How wonderful it would be to have kids like this. Kids who really cared about you.

"Okay," she sighed. "Just wait right here for a minute. I'll go get changed."

Hub went limp with relief as Aunt Grace hurried back to the house. He shifted to the passenger side, while Fat climbed into the back beside Pal.

"Nerves of steel," Fat said suddenly. "That's what Mr. Sutton said I needed, to stand on top of the pyramid. You got 'em too, Hub. I don't know how you had the guts to drive this jalopy."

"To tell you the truth, the thought of driving all the way to North Bridge scared me half to death," Hub confessed. "We'd probably never have made it in one piece. Either we'd have had an accident, or the cops would have nabbed us before we left town. Who knows, we might've had to spend the night in the pokey."

Half an hour later, as the car crept along the road, both boys were beginning to wonder if a night in jail might not have cost them less time than driving with Aunt Grace. They hadn't counted on their quick-witted aunt driving like a tortoise. How would they ever make it to Mom's place and back again in time for the Olympics?

"Can't you go any faster?" Hub blurted out.

Aunt Grace's hands were clenched around the steering wheel. "What if I drove over a poor little squirrel or a chipmunk? I'd never forgive myself."

"At the speed you're going, he'd have to be dead already for you to hit him!"

Grace shot him a look. Didn't he know what an effort it was for her to climb back into this deadly machine? She was only doing it for his sake, and Fat's. Honey's too, of course.

Reluctantly, she shifted into third, frowning through the windshield, trying to concentrate on the road ahead. North Bridge seemed so far away.

She leaned forward, peering. What was that in the distance? It was a man, that's what it was. A man wearing a brown suit, keeping well to the side of the road. A bulky man with a hat, carrying a briefcase. Oh my God. It was *her* man. It was her dream. All over again but different.

"Hey!" Fat pointed. "There's Judd. Judd Wainwright! Let's pick him up!"

Where was her best hat with the cherry-colored veil when she needed it? She hoped her hair looked halfway decent. Oh God, her nose! Was it shiny? Trying to glance in the rearview mirror, she pressed her foot accidentally on the accelerator. The car jumped forward, sped up and screeched to a stop beside Judd. Flustered, Grace rested her hand on the horn. It would have been hard to say who was more startled, Grace, the boys, or the unsuspecting salesman.

"Grace Bailey!" Judd stared past Hub to where she sat, proudly now, in the driver's seat. She smiled with delight. This was so much better than any dream. "I didn't know you could drive," he said admiringly.

"She can't," Hub answered. "She's driving this jalopy like a horse and buggy."

But Grace felt too happy to take offence. "What are you doing here, Judd?" she asked. "What a coincidence, running into you like this!"

He gazed at her, his round face nearly filling the passenger window. "I just sold a dozen novelty neckties to some crazy old coot living over on Route Seven. Thought I'd hitchhike to the next bus stop on the way to North Bridge."

"North Bridge—that's exactly where we're headed," she said, unable to believe her luck. Then, feeling impossibly daring, she asked, "Can I give you a life? I ... I mean ... a lift?"

He smiled, dazzling her. "Why sure, Gracie. I'd take either with you."

He had opened the rear door and was climbing inside when Grace started up the car again. The engine sputtered to life, then instantly lost interest.

"Good Lord!" Grace sighed, scarlet with embarrassment. "I wish I could pretend to be a competent driver. But I'm not."

Judd closed the rear door and walked around to her side. "You're probably just tired," he said mildly. "You've had a lot on your plate recently, Gracie. Why don't you allow me to drive the rest of the way?"

She felt her eyes fill with unexpected tears. He was so kind, so understanding. No one else ever seemed to take her feelings into account.

"Go ahead and drive, Judd," Hub was saying. "We were afraid Aunt Grace would take all night to get to North Bridge."

Grace bit back a retort and slid demurely over to the passenger seat, while the boys squabbled in the back about who got to sit next to Pal. Judd squeezed in beside Grace and took the wheel. She thanked her lucky stars that North Bridge was still another couple of hours away.

Under Judd's competent handling the car started up straight away. He eased it smoothly out into the road. In the back the boys had put Pal in the middle between them, and a companionable silence settled over them.

"Would you like me to give you a few driving tips, Gracie?" Judd offered. His smile warmed her through and through.

He is *a dream*, she thought. *Only much, much better.*

CHAPTER FIFTEEN

The light was just beginning to fade when the Ford pulled up outside Joe Callaghan's old rooming house. Honey had been sitting out on the fire escape mending one of her stockings, taking advantage of the last of the sun's rays, when she looked up and saw the car. Her darning still in her hand, she raced down the steps and flung her arms around the two boys.

"I can't believe it! I can't believe it!" she cried. "You're here! You came after all!"

She could have hugged the two of them forever, feeling the ache in her heart diminish. She kissed them and straightened up, forcing back the tears of relief. The last thing she wanted to do was upset her kids. She hardly spared a glance for the man in the driver's seat, thinking at first it was Bob Bailey. But a much larger man than Bob emerged from the car. He wore an ill-fitting suit and seemed slightly awkward, but he had the kindest of smiles and his face lit up when he looked at Grace.

"Honey, I want you to meet Judd. Judd Wainwright, my ... um ... an old school friend," Grace said, blushing.

"Delighted to meet you, Mr. Wainwright," Honey replied, shaking his hand warmly. "Now come on up, all of you. I'm sure you must be fainting with hunger after that long trip."

In the kitchen, preparing sandwiches, she could feel Grace's nervousness. Forgetting her own worries, she tried to put her sister-in-law at ease.

"He seems like a lovely man, that Judd Wainwright," she began. "Where've you been hiding him?"

"No place, really." Grace trimmed the crusts from the sandwiches with the utmost care. "We went out together once or twice, centuries ago, when I was in high school. And um ... and then—"

"No, let me guess," Honey interrupted. "Your mother didn't approve?"

"No ... well ..." Grace frowned at the sand-wiches. She hated to criticize her mother to anyone but herself.

Honey poured root beer into glasses. "If I were you I wouldn't let her stop me from seeing him." She glanced over at Grace. "I think he's a perfect gentleman."

A look of delight flashed over Grace. "You do? Really?"

"Of course I do." Honey felt a surge of affection for this woman who had stood by her through so much. "I want to thank you for bringing the boys here this weekend, Grace. I was dying to see them. But I can imagine how reluctant you must've felt to go near that car after the accident."

Grace put the sandwiches on a plate. "I had no choice. The boys made me come." She smiled. "They were worried about you. And so was I."

Through the open kitchen door she could see the boys in the living room playing cards with Judd. *Little pitchers have big ears*, she warned her-self. She moved closer to Honey.

"What happened, Honey?" she asked quietly. "You sounded so upset on the phone last night."

The tears, so long held back, gleamed in Honey's eyes. "I ... I lost my job yesterday," she blurted. "I didn't want to talk about it over the phone. But I've been so worried. If I don't pay this new rent increase next week the bank could throw me out of here. I don't know what to do, Grace! I was thinking maybe I should move to Toronto, to look for work."

"Toronto? But what about the boys?" The happiness Grace had carried inside her all afternoon was buried under this sudden new concern. Pity for Honey filled her. Putting her arms around her sister-in-law, she let her cry her fill. Over Honey's shoulder she saw Hub appear in the doorway, alerted by the sound of sobbing. Fat leant against him, looking close to tears himself. *They shouldn't have to witness such things at their age*, she thought protectively. But there was nothing she could do.

"I thought ... maybe I could go on Relief," Honey ventured, unaware that the boys were listening. "You don't get much money on Relief, I know. But it would help me find a room somewhere. Only it wouldn't be someplace I could bring the boys. There just aren't any jobs in North Bridge, Grace. I thought maybe I'd have better luck in Toronto."

Grace was shocked that Honey was considering taking government assistance. Why, if her mother found out, she would never let her forget it. "You know how much you'd get on Relief?" she asked. "No more than ten dollars. Ten dollars a month. Maybe less."

"You're not going on Relief," Hub said loudly, stepping into the room. "And you're not going to Toronto."

He'd been waiting all evening to tell his mom about the prize money. If ever there was a perfect moment, this was it. Stepping forward, he pulled out his ace and slammed it down. "We're planning to win some prize money at the Boys' Olympics, Mom. It's a lot of money. And we're gonna give you all our share."

"Oh, Hub ..." Honey's tears still fell, but she was smiling now. She drew both boys to her in a hug. "What would I do without you guys?"

It was then that Grace suddenly remembered the twenty-five dollars her mother had given her to pay Mr. Jefferson's bill. "Hub's absolutely right, Honey," she cried, dashing to grab her purse from the kitchen table. "You are not going on Relief and that is that." Taking the money from her wallet, she handed it to Honey. "Here, take it. Twenty-five dollars to tide you over until you get another job. Go on, I mean it."

Honey backed away, shaking her head. "No! I can't take your money, Grace!"

It's not my money! Grace almost said. But she

stopped in time. Honey would never take it if she knew it belonged to May Bailey.

"I will not take no for an answer!" she said instead, scowling and thrusting the money into her sister-in-law's apron pocket.

It made Honey laugh. "You're such a doll," she cried, throwing her arms around Grace. "Okay. I'll accept this as a loan. I'll pay you back, every single cent, I promise."

"I know you will." Grace picked up the plate of sandwiches and plonked them on the kitchen table. "Okay, everybody!" she called. "Let's eat!"

The room erupted into happy confusion. The boys ran about looking for enough chairs to seat everyone. Pal darted between people's feet, his tail wagging furiously. Barking, he put his paws on the table and tried to nuzzle the sandwiches, while Honey batted him away with a napkin, laughing and teasing him, her face still wet with tears. In the living room, Judd wound up the Victrola and suddenly music filled the apartment—a sweet, jazzy tune that made Grace's feet itch to dance.

"May I have the pleasure of this dance, Miss Bailey?"

Judd stood beaming in the doorway, one hand extended towards her. It seemed to her as if the room suddenly fell silent.

"Oh n-no," she stammered. "I think ... really ... I think we should probably eat."

Honey pushed Grace gently forward towards Judd. "Go on and dance, Grace. Don't be a party pooper."

Grace felt suspended, slightly curious—as though her life were about to change and she could do absolutely nothing either to advance or slow that change.

"Go on," Honey said again. "Dance, for heaven's sake."

Judd stood very still. Stepping forward Grace took his hand. Slowly they began to move to the music, circling together in their first dance.

CHAPTER SIXTEEN

A thin mist hung low to the ground as the two boys and Grace set out very early the next morning on their drive back to New Bedford. The air had a chilly bite. It reminded Hub that fall was on its way. Would they be together again as a family by the time winter came? He hoped so, desperately.

When they did leave their grandmother's

house, though, he would miss Aunt Grace. He looked over at her fondly as they drove along. Her grip on the wheel seemed more relaxed. She was humming quietly to herself. He remembered how she had handed the money over to Mom last night. Impulsively. As if she simply couldn't stand by and watch another person suffer. She was a good person, Aunt Grace. Not a mean bone in her body.

"What are you going to tell Grandmother about the car money, Aunt Grace?" he asked. He didn't want her getting into trouble.

She stopped humming and thought for a while. "Jeez. I don't know. I haven't figured that one out yet. I won't tell her I gave it to your mom, though."

"Well she won't hear it from us, either," Fat assured her.

Hub swiveled around to look at his brother in the back seat, and Fat nodded his agreement. They'd discussed something before they'd fallen asleep the night before. Hub turned back to Aunt Grace. "We could give you our share of the prize money once we've won. Mom doesn't need it so urgently now. You could give it to Grandmother. Or straight to Mr. Jefferson."

Grace smiled at them both. "That's very kind of you boys," she said. "But I'm not sure it'll solve my problem. It sure would be handy if she forgot she ever gave it to me. Wouldn't it be great if that bump on the head made her lose her memory?"

Ahead of them the road forked. Grace slowed from a creep to a crawl. "Oh dear," she muttered. "I don't remember any of these roads. I guess I ... I must have been a little distracted on our way up. I wasn't really paying much attention."

Hub stared at the two tree-lined roads curving away from each other. Neither had anything distinctive about it. He had no idea which was the right one. "That way," he said, pointing impulsively to the right. "That looks like the best way to go."

But the farther they drove along the road he had chosen, the worse its condition grew. Soon they were bumping along over logs roughly rolled together. "I swear this road hasn't been improved since the settlers built it," grumbled Aunt Grace. "They used to call it a 'corduroy road' because of all the ridges made by the logs."

The sun climbed higher in the sky. The chill of the morning had long evaporated, replaced by a mind-numbing heat. Soon even the logs gave out and the road tapered to a narrow muddy trail.

"This isn't even a road any more!" Fat complained, trying to fan himself with Pal's tail. "It's a swamp!"

Hub was just about to suggest they turn around and go back when the car backfired and shuddered to a halt.

"Blast it!" Grace gasped, losing her temper. "I must have been out of my cotton-picking mind to take that turn. What am I doing here anyway? I wish I'd never ever seen this confounded car in my whole life!" She jiggled the keys in the ignition, turning the engine off, then on. She pressed the starter button. Nothing happened.

Hub leaned over and studied the dashboard. "No wonder we stopped, Aunt Grace," he said finally. "The needle's on E."

"E? What's E supposed to mean?"

Fat groaned from the back seat. "E for Empty, Aunt Grace," he said loudly. "Empty as in all gone. No more. Bye, bye, gasoline."

Grace bent her head till it was resting on the steering wheel. "She'll never forgive me for stealing this car, let alone taking all that money. She'll hold this over my head for the rest of my life."

Hub put his arm around her shoulder. "It's okay, Aunt Grace. I think I saw a farm back there a ways. They might be able to spare us some gas. C'mon, Fat. Let's go."

But Grace was having none of it. "You think you're gonna walk away and leave me in this car alone? No way. This car is coming with us."

"You must be kidding!" Hub objected. "You want us to push this monstrosity backwards through the mud?"

"My mind's made up. I am not letting you or this car out of my sight!"

And so, with Fat steering, supervised by Pal, who sat nervously beside him in the passenger seat, Hub and Grace pushed the Ford back out of the swamp, down the corduroy road and into the farmer's front yard.

Luckily for them, the farmer was at home and happy to earn a few cents filling up their tank. Hub leaned against the headlights, feeling wretched.

"We'll never make it in time now," he mumbled to Fat. "We can kiss that prize money goodbye."

"What're we gonna do?" Fat rested his head in his hands, his elbows on the hood. "We promised that money to Mom. We're sunk, that's what we are."

Washing her hands at the nearby pump, Grace heard the hopelessness in Fat's voice. A light came into her eyes, the light of determination. She paid the farmer, thanked him politely and hopped back into the car.

"Climb in, let's go!" she called, honking the horn. "And don't look so glum. We're not beat yet!" Flexing her fingers, she started the car, letting the clutch out smoothly as she pressed her right foot down on the accelerator. The car purred into life, springing at the road like a hungry cat. "Wheeee!" Grace whooped. "Hang onto your hats, guys! This is gonna be fun!"

"Looks like Aunt Grace musta learned something from Judd's driving tips," Hub whispered to Fat. "She's going like a bat out of hell!"

It was true. Grace was flying along the road like a professional racing car driver. "Faint heart never won fair lady," she yelled over the throb of the motor. "Ever heard that expression before, guys? It means you gotta fight to win. Anyway, I've decided to stop worrying about Mother and her damn car, for the moment. It's all her fault we're in this mess anyway."

"How come?" queried Fat.

"Well, look at it this way: Mother sent your mom away, making it necessary for me to take you two to visit her every so often. Then she insisted on teaching me to drive, which landed her in the hospital and the car in hock to Mr. Jefferson. Then—"

"Look out, Aunt Grace!" Hub clutched the dashboard, sweaty with terror. "You almost killed that chipmunk!"

"Aw, what's a chipmunk or two in the grand scheme of things?" Grace swerved recklessly around a corner. Hub decided not to remind her of her earlier concern for four-footed furry creatures.

"The truck, Aunt Grace! Watch out!" shrieked Fat a moment later. A rickety farm truck was rattling towards them, taking up most of the road.

Aunt Grace leaned out the window. "Get a horse!" she hollered at the petrified driver, shaking her fist.

"There's no point in getting us all killed, Aunt Grace," Hub said, trying to sound matter-of-fact rather than just plain despairing. "We'll never make it now anyway."

"Sure we'll make it," cried Aunt Grace. "Or my name ain't Grace Bailey!"

"Yeah, well. We won't need names once we're dead," Fat replied gloomily.

His arm around Pal, he settled back to await his fate.

CHAPTER SEVENTEEN

So far, everything to do with the fall fair had fallen smoothly into place, Max Sutton reflected with some astonishment. The marquee had gone up without a hitch. Several stalls had been erected and were doing a brisk business, selling everything from preserves and jellies to miraculous cures and tonics. Brightly colored bunting and small Union Jacks stretched from stall to stall. A huge banner proclaiming the Boys' Olympics occupied pride of place at the entrance to the competition area.

People had come from miles around. Dressed in their holiday best, they sauntered around the field or lolled in the improvised bleachers, determined to enjoy the last public holiday of the summer. The enthusiastic volunteer band had struck up "Carolina Moon," and the lilting music set even the primmest of New Bedford's citizens to swaying and smiling.

Yes, so far, thought Max, everything was fine. But a nagging worry prevented him from relaxing and enjoying the occasion.

The voice of the school principal, Mr. Pagnutti, boomed through the megaphone. "In just a moment, the highlight of the Boys' Olympics, the Human Pyramid, will be taking place!"

There was a smattering of spontaneous applause.

Max's worry came into focus. That was it. The Bailey boys. He hadn't laid eyes on them since

Friday. He walked over to the sheltered corner where Tony Piretti and Buck Mayhew were organizing the New Bedford team. Tony had chosen the spot himself, anxious to avoid for as long as possible being seen by Mr. Pagnutti or Mr. Grady.

"Hey, Buck," Mr. Sutton asked. "Have you seen Hub or Fat?"

"Ain't seen 'em all day," Buck replied.

Max scratched his head. This was so unlike the Baileys. Both of them had seemed genuinely keen on the Olympics. Where the heck were they? He thought for a moment. "I guess there's no chance the Doogans will turn up, eh?"

"About as much chance as a snowball's in Hell, I'd say! You think ol' man Doogan's gonna let those guys outta his sight?" Tony asked incredulously. He stepped away from the others, drawing Max with him. "Say, Coach." His voice sank to a whisper. "I'm worried about this dangblasted pyramid. I don't think these guys can do it. The crowd's making 'em nervous."

Max, studying Tony's serious face, was pleased to see the boy's newfound sense of responsibility. It strengthened his resolve to maintain the athletics club, no matter what the Gradys of this world said against it.

"I guess we have to allow for the fact that the

Baileys may not turn up," he said to Tony. "I need you to look around for someone about Fat's size to crown the pyramid. The rest of you will just have to rearrange yourselves from the base up. Try putting Sam on the bottom, instead of Buck."

"Sure thing, Coach." Tony turned away to begin the search. "Don't worry," he added, over his shoulder. "These things have a way of working out."

"Do your best, okay, fellas?" Max called out to the rest of the athletes. He checked his watch. "I gotta go now and announce the Pinebury team."

Signaling to the band to hold their fire, Max stepped up onto the announcer's platform. He nodded to Mr. Pagnutti and spoke clearly into the megaphone. "And now, please welcome the team from Pinebury, sponsored by Pinebury Auto Body."

He watched as the Pinebury boys ran onto the field in their white team shirts, took up their positions and assembled their pyramid with precision and efficiency. "They're good," he muttered to Pagnutti, his heart sinking a little. "Damn good."

"A big round of applause for the team from Pinebury!" he called later as the boy at the top knelt upright, throwing his arms in the air, supported by a resolutely unwobbling base.

The crowd cheered. With all its economy of

movement, the Pinebury team disassembled itself, bowed and dispersed.

Max felt worry deepen to alarm. After the Golden team it would be New Bedford's turn. "Now ladies and gentlemen," he called out, "a warm round of applause for the Golden team."

In the meantime Tony had spotted Squinty Moore, youngest brother of an old friend of his, Frankie-the-Fingers Moore, famed far and wide for his ability to lift the change out of a man's pockets without his victim feeling a thing. Fingers was doing serious time in jail, but Tony recognized Squinty straight away as a chip off the old block. It wasn't just the squint, although crossed eyes seemed to run in the Moore family. It was the way he held his hands, cradling them in front of his chest, as though to shelter them from harm. If those fingers were even half as talented as Frankie's, they had to be worth their weight in gold.

"Hey!" He stopped in front of Squinty, a runty kid in a grubby undershirt. "You're a Moore, ain'tcha?"

Squinty immediately shoved his hands in his pockets. He nodded. His head was down. Strands of greasy brown hair hid his eyes.

"How's Fingers?"

"Ain't seen mucha him lately." Squinty spoke without lifting his head.

"Howdya like the opportunity of a lifetime, kid? The chance to be top banana in our pyramid. Whaddya say?"

Squinty thrust his hands deeper into his pockets. He spoke to the ground. "Ain't too bad with heights," he mumbled. "Ever since Frankie got took, I been practicin' on the drainpipe outside my window."

Already Tony was pushing him towards the New Bedford group. "You'll get a brand new shirt for your trouble."

Squinty stopped abruptly and inspected the grass. "A new shirt?" Deep in his pants pockets, his hands twitched. "Ain't got no shirt at all right now," he told the grass. "Sure could do with a clean one. All I got is this." He jerked his chin downwards towards his soiled undershirt.

"You wanna give it a try?" Tony asked.

Squinty nodded slowly, his eyes examining a healthy-looking thistle. "Guess so. Guess I'll need a clean shirt." He raised his head. His squint was truly terrible. "What if someone steps on my hands?"

"No one's gonna step on your hands, kid." Tony patted the greasy head gingerly. "Don't you worry."

He was in the middle of explaining to Squinty how he should go about climbing to the top of the pyramid when he heard a hoarse holler. The three Doogan brothers came lumbering across the field towards him. His spirits rose.

"What happened? You lock your dad in the outhouse or what?"

"We ran like the hammers of hell," gasped Sean.

"Are we too late?" panted Quinn.

"Not if you get a move on. Come on, quick. Hey, Sam! Help me stuff these guys into jerseys!"

Everyone cooperated in helping the Doogans get dressed. "You know somethin'?" Tony confided to the brothers. "If your ol' man could let you take part in this, maybe, just maybe, we got a fightin' chance. 'Specially now we got Squinty here. Say, where'd that kid go?"

Looking around, he saw Squinty squatting on the grass, one precious hand tucked carefully under his arm. He had released the other from confinement and now ran his fingers lightly over the new team shirt, stroking it, as if unable to believe this bright clean garment had really become part of his own wardrobe.

The canary yellow of the shirt did nothing for Squinty's complexion. He looked even weedier and runtier than before. No matter how hard he tried, Tony couldn't imagine him triumphing at the top of their pyramid. He thought wistfully of the sturdy, energetic Bailey boy. "Where in blazes is that pip-squeak, Fat?" he muttered savagely.

"Hey, ease up, Piretti!" Buck was staring at him in disbelief. "You used ta be Mr. Tough Guy, remember? You never got worked up over nothin'. How come you're taking things so serious all of a sudden?"

"It's sixty bucks, ain't it?" Tony snapped.

But it wasn't the money, not really. He'd never been part of something like this before. Something normal and special at the same time. It made him feel that maybe, if he tried real hard this time, he could belong.

A roar of laughter went up suddenly from the crowd. Peering round the nearest stall, Tony saw the Golden team's pyramid had collapsed into a jumble.

"A big hand for the team from Golden." Max's voice rang out over the boisterous crowd.

"Hell's bells! It's our turn next! We're on next!" Tony whispered in a sudden panic. He'd have to face the crowd. Hundreds of staring faces. Faces that could boo or hiss as well as cheer. Mr. Pagnutti would be there. And so would Mr. Grady.

"And now, thanks to the generosity of the *New Bedford Weekly Chronicle*, we present New Bedford's pride and joy, the New Bedford Athletics Club!"

The band struck up. The crowd roared its approval.

"We're on!" whispered Buck. "Good luck, everyone!"

Tony saw that Buck's eyes were shining. *He's just as serious about this as me*, he realized with astonishment. *Only he don't have as much to lose if things go wrong*.

Somehow this thought gave him courage. Pushing Squinty Moore ahead of him, he led the team out onto the field. Applause thundered around him. Shoulders back, head erect, he took his place at the center of the field. The others positioned themselves around him.

"We're gonna win!" he whispered to Buck. "We're gonna win those sixty smackers!"

Kneeling down, he looked the crowd over for the first time, and found himself staring straight into the hostile eyes of his old nemesis, Alastair Grady.

CHAPTER EIGHTEEN

Fat clicked open the suitcase he shared with Hub and rooted wildly inside. Clothes flew out all over the back seat of the car. Where oh where was his doggone shirt?

"I can't find it!" he yelled. "My official team shirt ain't here!"

Pal poked his nose into the case and lifted several garments up in the air as though trying to help Fat. Suppressing an urge to burst out crying, Fat threw himself on Pal and buried his face in the dog's warm coat. What did it matter if he found it anyway? They were never going to get there in time.

"Two minutes! We'll be there in two minutes, I promise you," Aunt Grace called from the front. "We'll be right at the school!"

Oh sure, Aunt Grace.

Why did everything have to go wrong, he wondered? Ever since Dad died, nothing had gone their way. That day Tony had picked him to be top of the pyramid, he'd thought then that maybe things were going to get better. They might have, too. If only their team could have won the prize money.

Hub was keeping very quiet in the front seat.

Fat felt sure his big brother was thinking the exact same thing he was. They were gonna let Mom down.

"We're here!" Grace called, squealing to a stop beside the school playing field.

"Come on, Pal. Let's go!" Fat yelled, leaping out of the car. Hub was ahead of him, racing towards the crowd.

"Come back, Hub! You forgot your shirt!" called Aunt Grace.

She hadn't noticed that Fat didn't have his shirt either. But as he dashed towards the bleachers, he could see he wasn't going to need it. The New Bedford team was already out on the field. There they were, resplendent in their yellow shirts with "NEW BEDFORD" in bold green letters across the front and "CHRONICLE" on the back. He could see Tony Piretti holding his own at the base of the pyramid. Higher up, Buck and the others were keeping the second row steady. And now the third layer was climbing into place. All that was needed was the kingpin. The guy at the top. Should he race out and take his rightful place, Fat wondered? What did it matter if he didn't have the right shirt on? Everyone knew he belonged at the top.

But no. Someone else was already clambering up the backs of the bottom line of pyramid-builders. A kid with greasy hair. A runty-looking weedy little squirt who looked like he had no hands! For the love of Pete! The runt was stumbling up the pyramid, hands in his pockets, kneeing and elbowing and toeing his way up! He was good, a good climber. Only why in the name of all that's holy didn't he take his goldang hands out of his drawers?

In spite of everything, Fat found himself rooting for the weird kid. Already he'd wriggled his way to the top of the second layer. Up he went again. Now he had one foot on the backs of the top row and—

"Look out!" Fat couldn't stop himself from yelling. Unable to rectify his stumble, due to his hands being out on strike, the boy lost his footing and went tumbling down, down, down into a great puddle of whipped up grass and dirt. A fatal wobble rippled like a breeze through the pyramid. The wobble spread to a gust. The gust whipped itself up into a whirlwind of arms, heads, shoes, legs. The pyramid blew away.

A collective groan escaped from the crowd in the improvised stands.

"We lost!" Hub said softly, a look of devastation on his face.

"What happened? What happened?" Aunt Grace came running up behind them, Hub's shirt in her hand. She stopped, listening, as Mr. Sutton's voice blared from the megaphone.

"The winner of the Human Pyramid competition is the team from Pinebury." He sounded detached, impartial. How could he sound that way, Fat wondered, when he'd promised Mr. Cramp the New Bedford team would win? How could he sound so cool, when the fate of his athletics club hung in the balance?

"I'd like to thank all those who participated," Mr. Sutton continued calmly. "The junior egg-and-spoon race will take place two minutes from now. Once again, congratulations, Pinebury!"

To the strains of the victory march from *Aida* and the applause of the crowd, the Pinebury team reappeared on the field to take its bows.

"Aw nuts!" Hub stamped the ground in frustration. "It was all for nothing!"

Fat's bottom lip quivered. "Being top of the pyramid was the only thing I was ever any good at," he said in a low voice.

"We'd have won if you'd been on top, Fat," Hub told him.

"You think so? Really?" Maybe it wasn't even true, but it sure was nice of Hub to say something like that.

Fat wasn't the only one who felt he'd let the side

down. It had been Hub who'd suggested they take that wrong turn. And he'd been the one who'd insisted on going to North Bridge to check up on Mom in the first place. Well, at least they'd seen Mom. Even if they hadn't won any prize money for her. At least they'd cheered her up a little.

Aunt Grace seemed to be thinking along the same lines. "Listen to me, boys," she was saying. "We're here now. Okay, so we missed the competition. But we might as well make the best of the rest of the day. That'd make your Mom happy, you know—just to think you boys had a good time." She handed the yellow shirt to Hub. "C'mon. Put this on right now. Yours is in the car, Fat. I saw it on the ledge behind the back seat. Go get your team colors on and have a ball."

Fat made his way back to the car. He was just reaching into the back seat for his shirt when he heard a muffled sob. He closed the door softly and looked around for the source of the sound.

Sitting by the trunk of the Ford, his head between his knees, the greasy-haired kid who'd fallen off the top of the pyramid sobbed as though his life were over. His hands were still not in evidence. Up close, Fat could see their outline buried deep in the pockets of his pants.

"Hey, what's up?" Fat crouched beside him.

Startled, the kid looked up. One eye stared straight at Fat; the other careened off towards the street. Tears coursed down his thin face, mingling with the dust and grime on his cheeks. His nose ran. He was not a pretty sight.

"I got my new shirt all mucked up," he said, wiping his nose on his bare arm. He dropped his chin down onto his yellow New Bedford team shirt, and Fat saw that it was stained all over with grass and dirt and the imprint of the shoes of many fallen pyramid-builders.

"Can't you ask your mom to wash it for you?" Fat asked.

Tears sprang again to his eyes. "Don't got no mom," he muttered. "I got one brother, see? An' he's in jail." Carefully, he removed his hands from his pockets to rub his tears away. Fat saw that they were white and fine-boned, with thin, sensitive fingers.

"You've got nice hands." It was a statement more than a compliment.

A slow smile stole some of the sadness from the boy's face. He held his hands in front of his squint, gazing at them lovingly. "These hands is my inheritance," he said, pride strengthening his voice. "That's what Frankie says. They're my livelihood, see? Soon's they got me set up, like in business, they're gonna help me break Frankie outta the pokey."

"Wow!" Fat didn't quite understand, but he was impressed. "You play the piano, eh? Is that what you do?" Fat loved anything to do with performing. "Do you get to go on stages? In front of audiences?"

"The pianny? Are you kiddin'? Wouldn't touch them things. Them things is death on the fingers. No," he said haughtily. "Safe-crackin's my game. Squinty's the name."

"I'm Henry. But everyone calls me Fat. Fat Bailey." Fat held out his hand politely, but Squinty shook his head.

"Put that thing away," he commanded. "I never shake hands neither. Too dangerous."

He cuddled his hands against his chest, like delicate white birds. "I was plannin' to visit Frankie, " he confided. "Check out the locks on his cell, see? Thought I'd be a real mickey-dazzler in this shirt. And now, look at the cut of me. He'd be ashamed to see me the way I am." Tears welled in his eyes once more. "He's a stickler for cleanliness, is our Frankie. Can't abide dirt."

Fat had a sudden inspiration. "Take mine," he said, holding out his team shirt. "I haven't even worn it yet."

Squinty blinked at him. "You mean, you'd give me the shirt off your back?"

"It's not on my back."

Squinty took the shirt reverently, framing it in his beautiful hands.

"You'd better wash yourself first, before you put it on," Fat advised. "There's a pump down there, near the marquee."

"I won't forget this," Squinty said slowly. "I won't forget what you done, Fat Bailey. If ever you need a safe cracked, you just call on me, Squinty Moore, you hear?"

That encounter with Squinty made Fat feel better. At least he still had a mother, he reflected, watching Squinty's thin frame scurry towards the pump. And a brother who wasn't in jail.

CHAPTER NINETEEN

Max groaned inwardly as he saw Mr. Grady and Mr. Cramp marching in his direction. Alastair Grady's heavy bulldog face looked as though a bone had stuck in his gullet.

"What the devil's going on, Sutton?" he barked. "I thought I had that ruffian Piretti expelled from school. And there he was on our team, large as life and twice as ugly!"

"I take full responsibility for his presence," Max shot back. "Tony did a fine job. I've no complaints about him."

"I'm the one with the complaints!" Mr. Cramp waved an unlit cigar at Max. "Think of the money I sank into that publicity campaign! You assured me that team of yours was going to win, Sutton!"

Over the publisher's shoulder, across a field now littered with overturned chairs and limp balloons, Max saw a bloated figure puffing towards them. It was Mr. Doogan. He was waving his arms about and muttering incoherently. Max resigned himself to another volley of complaints.

"Hey, Sutton!" Mr. Doogan bellowed. "I gotta talk to you!"

"You're going to have to stand in line, Mr. Doogan."

Doogan looked taken aback. "Ain't gonna take that long. I just wanna thank you, sir!" He reached for Max's hand. "I wanna thank you from the bottom of my heart."

"You want to ... *thank* me?" Max couldn't believe his ears.

"Them boys of mine hayed them fields so fast, they'd take the sight from your eyes!" Bursting with enthusiasm, Doogan turned to the newspaper publisher and the school trustee. "This um ... at-lettuce thing, now ..."

"The athletics program?" Max prompted. He'd never seen Doogan so animated.

"Yup, that's it. This at-lettuce program of yours. Best thing that ever happened to my boys. A beautiful thing, that's what it is, for the school. Wouldn't you agree, Cramp?" Doogan poked a fervent elbow into Cramp's belly. The cigar flew out of the publisher's mouth, which remained molded in an O of surprise.

Max stooped to recover the cigar and returned it to the newspaper man, who held it to his nose shortsightedly, inspecting it for dirt.

"I'm sorry to say, Mr. Doogan, that Mr. Grady here has seen fit to cut athletics from the school curriculum." It had suddenly occurred to Max that Doogan, in his present exalted condition, might make a fuss. He prayed he would. And to his delight, Doogan obliged.

"Well, now, isn't that a shame!" Mr. Doogan looked Mr. Grady up and down coldly. "'Tis a shame when money gets to be more important than the good of children. Anyone who'd put dough ahead of kids is low, very low. Lower than a flounder, I'd say."

Grady said nothing; he merely showed his teeth in a snarl.

Warming to his theme, Doogan rocked back on his heels. "I'd say I wouldn't be the only parent thinkin' that way, neither. I'd say most of the folks involved in this here Olympics would fight to keep their kids doin' them at ... at-lettuce-isms." The burly farmer turned towards Mr. Cramp. "You bein' a man of education, I'm sure you'd agree with me, Cramp. After all, you're the one we have to thank for supporting our kids from the beginning. I'm on my way down to your office now, so I am, to renew my subscription to your newspaper. An' I've told every one of my neighbors in the fields beyond to do the same thing. You done a great thing, Cramp. A noble thing." Moved by his own rhetoric, Mr. Doogan pulled out a grubby handkerchief and blew his bulbous nose.

Mr. Cramp gazed from Mr. Doogan to Mr. Grady and back to Max Sutton. Wiping the cigar with his tie, he popped it in his mouth. His moon face wrinkled in thought. "Well ... uh ..." he said, finally. "I guess I always believed in *mens sana in corpore sano*, don't you know."

"Huh? What's that when it's at home?" Mr. Doogan asked.

"A healthy mind in a healthy body," translated Max.

"My thoughts exactly!" agreed the farmer. He pumped Mr. Cramp's hand up and down. "An' I'm sure every single one of the other parents would say the very same thing: Mensana manana and so on. Hell of an expression. Put that on the front page, why don't you!" As he turned to leave, he slapped Max Sutton on the back. "You're a good man, too, Sutton," he boomed. "May you be in heaven half an hour before the Devil knows you're dead!"

As Doogan turned to leave, his muddy boots landed heavily on top of Mr. Grady's gleaming shoes. Mr. Grady let out a yelp of anguish and hopped up and down, grasping at his wounded feet and sputtering with fury.

Catching him up with both hands, Doogan lifted the school trustee off his feet and set him down again to rights on the grass. "There," he said. "Gotta keep things in balance, right Alastair? Now don't be such a hard nut. Them boys had a heck of a great time! Money ain't everything, you know. Not by a long shot."

Max Sutton stared after the departing Doogan. Who'd have thought Doogan, of all people, would come to his defense?

Mr. Cramp broke into a guffaw. "'Which only goes to show you that it pays to advertise!'" he quoted as he lit his cigar. "Money well spent, that's what I say!"

But Alastair Grady shook his doggy jowls. "This isn't over, Sutton!" he snapped, wiping his shoes on the grass. "If I get my hands on that Piretti kid ... I ... I won't be responsible for my actions!"

He hobbled off across the field as though determined to find Tony Piretti himself and strangle him with his bare hands.

CHAPTER TWENTY

After the collapse of the New Bedford pyramid, Tony did his best to stay out of sight. The shock of being caught in full public view in the spotlight of Mr. Grady's glare brought home to him just how much trouble he was in.

He'd never really planned to set the school trustee's shed on fire. It was one of those things that seemed to happen almost spontaneously. He and his buddies had been out trick-or-treating on Hallowe'en. On that night the streets were almost always deserted, except for gangs of rowdy kids eager to play tricks on people who refused to "treat" them. Knocking over outdoor privies was a favorite sport—particularly if the owner was still inside. So when Mr. Grady slammed his front door in the faces of Tony and his pals, they'd gone hunting for his outhouse.

Unfortunately for them, the school trustee was one of the few people in the area who had installed one of those newfangled indoor toilets. His shed had seemed the next best target. But when the kids had crowded round the small, pristine new building, all attempts to lift it off the ground failed. Mr. Grady's shed, they saw, was firmly attached to a concrete base. No amount of huffing and puffing was going to overturn it. That's when Buck had made his fateful dare.

"Go on," he'd said, staring straight at Tony. "Dare ya ta torch it!"

And Tony, stupidly, had bitten.

At that moment, Tony's prospects had gone up in flames. Just like the shed. All hell had broken loose. Turned out Mr. Grady had been watching them from his darkened bedroom window the whole time. He'd seen Tony place the gasoline-soaked rag in the doorway and set it alight. Grady punished Tony by having him expelled from school. But the punishment that Tony called down on himself was worse: he had to live with the knowledge that he'd burnt all the bridges between himself and any successful, grown-up life.

When Hub had asked him to participate in Mr. Sutton's athletics club, it was the first time in almost a year that Tony had felt any hope—hope that maybe someday he could stop being an exile and become accepted again. For him, an end to the athletics program meant an end to his hopes for the future.

It was too early to go home. Instead he hung about the stalls, hiding in corners, watching the passers-by. They seemed so sure of themselves, so carefree, they made him envious.

Noticing Fat Bailey signing up for one of the competitions, Tony sneaked over to join him. Fat was standing at a table beside a row of sweet-smelling fruit pies.

Fat turned red with embarrassment when he saw Tony. "Sorry about missing the Human Pyramid, Piretti," he mumbled.

"Some mean trick," snapped the older boy. "We mighta won if you'd been there."

That was what Hub had said, too, Fat remembered, and he couldn't help feeling just a little pleased, despite his discomfort. "Anyway, it's not whether you win or lose, right, Tony? It's ..."

He waited for Tony to finish the phrase, but Tony stared at him with sleepy, puzzled eyes.

"Whaddya mean? You sayin' losin' don't matter none?"

"That's what they say. They say it's how you play the game that counts." He smiled up at the somber Tony. "I think you played the game real well."

Tony stopped himself just in time from smiling back. "Thanks, kid," was all he said.

Fat could tell he was pleased. "You wanna join the pie-eating competition, Tony?" he asked now. "I'm the only one signed up. It's just me against Arabella so far."

Tony looked around for Fat's competitor but could see no one. "A dame, eh?" He smoothed his hair back. Tony fancied himself a bit of a ladies' man. "So where is she?"

"Right there." Fat pointed.

Looking down, Tony saw an enormous pink pig ogling a fruit pie placed tantalizingly in front of her. Arabella's owner, a severe-looking woman in a dark suit and hat, stood behind her. She had tied a thick velvet ribbon around Arabella's neck and was now pulling on it with all her might to restrain the sow from diving snout first into the pie.

"Are you ready, Mrs. Schweinbach?" the judge asked.

Mrs. Schweinbach pulled the net down from her hat, hooked it under her nose, tightened her hold on Arabella's restraint and nodded.

"Ready, Fat?"

Fat grinned at Tony. "Always ready for pie," he whispered. "Ready, Miss Dahlberg!" he called to the judge, an apple-cheeked old lady, all decked out in pioneer garb.

"On your marks, get set, go!" the pioneer called, blowing her whistle loudly.

Mrs. Schweinbach released the ribbon. Arabella shot forward, skidded into the plate and began rooting around in the pastry, snuffling in ecstasy.

"That's it, Arabella! Eat, girl! Eat!" her owner screeched.

The small circle of onlookers tightened as more and more people gathered behind them, attracted by the encouraging shrieks of Mrs. Schweinbach. Tony didn't dare cheer for Fat. He didn't want people noticing him. But Fat, he saw, was doing all right. His head was buried in the pastry, his eyes were closed, his jaws working overtime. He looked, Tony thought with a grin, happy as a pig in pie.

Without noticing, Tony had moved forward into the center of the circle, where Fat and Arabella held the public's gaze. All of a sudden, he felt someone touch his elbow. With a start, he turned, and saw Mr. Sutton.

"Better watch out for Grady," Mr. Sutton murmured. "He's on the warpath."

Tony glanced about him quickly, but could see no sign of the school trustee. "Guess this means the end of the athletics program, eh, Coach?" He wanted to add, "And of me." But he couldn't bring himself to bare his soul that way.

To his surprise Mr. Sutton shook his head. "Not if Mr. Doogan has anything to do with it," he answered, a smile lighting his dark eyes. "Or Mr. Cramp, for that matter. I'd say the program has a pretty healthy chance. And I want you to be part of it, Piretti. I think you have a bright future as a coach. You're good with young kids, I've noticed."

Max's eyes had been scanning the crowd as he spoke. Beyond the nearest row of onlookers, he caught sight of Alastair Grady, pushing his way through the crowd. Tightening his hold on Tony's elbow, Max grabbed his head with the other hand and shoved him down under the table. "Get down and stay down," he hissed. "Until I give you the all clear."

Tony found himself crouched beside Arabella.

Mr. Sutton's words rang in his ears. "I've got a future after all," he confided dreamily to the pig. "He said so, a bright one!"

One of Arabella's ears twitched. But she appeared uninterested in Tony's future, no matter how bright. Jellied strawberries hung like jewels from her jowls. Her front paws scrabbled at a large circle of pineapple which she appeared to be trying to inhale through her snout.

"Go, Arabella, GOBBLE! GOBBLE! GOBBLE!" howled Mrs. Schweinbach.

But in the end it was Fat who won the contest. It didn't hurt that he hadn't eaten since leaving North Bridge. He'd been so famished he could have swallowed the dish as well. Luckily for its owner, Miss Dahlberg had blown her whistle as he was licking the last of the fruit away from the sides. Arabella's plate was still rotating noisily. Round and round it went, as the pig ignored the rest of her pastry, hypnotized by the revolving golden circle on the end of her nose.

"Dirty, stupid sow!" wept Mrs. Schweinbach. "Use yer teeth, can'tcha. Not yer snout!"

But Arabella was a lost cause. Fat had beaten her to the finish line. The crowd applauded and stamped as Miss Dahlberg awarded him a silver dollar. Refusing to congratulate the winner, Mrs.

Schweinbach stalked off in a huff, leaving Arabella to finish dining alone.

Aunt Grace's face was wreathed in smiles. So was Hub's. "I told you, you should just concentrate on what you do best," he grinned at his brother, flinging an arm around his shoulder. "Come on, let's go see Grandmother in the hospital."

The three of them tramped off to the pump first, so Hub could wash his fruit-stained face. They didn't notice Tony, who had fallen asleep beside Arabella. The perplexed pig didn't notice him either. She was too busy trying to grasp the pineapple dangling from her snout like an unattainable moon. Her frustrated snuffling failed to disturb Tony. For the first time in almost a year, he slept soundly.

Under the white tablecloth he was dreaming of his future, and its brightness dazzled him.

CHAPTER TWENTY-ONE

The sun was setting as they reached the hospital. No one seemed to be around at that hour, and they made their way to Mrs. Bailey's room through a silent corridor, dappled with shadowy light.

Her eyes closed, May lay still against the pillows. *How pale she is*, thought Grace. *White on white*.

With her silver hair set off by the snowy lace collar at her throat, Mrs. Bailey had the appearance of an antique, porcelain doll, fragile and vulnerable. Grace wasn't used to thinking of her mother in those terms, and it made her feel uncomfortable. For the first time, it dawned on Grace that one of these days her mother might really become dependent on her.

Let me be good to her when the time comes, she prayed. *Patient and kind. Not bossy, like her. Don't let me turn into her, Lord. Please.*

As if stirred by her daughter's prayer, Mrs. Bailey opened her eyes. "There you are," she said weakly. "I'm so glad you finally came. That nurse gave me so much medication, I couldn't remember when you were last here."

Grace blinked. Did that mean Mother had forgotten about Mr. Jefferson's twenty-five dollars?

"I'm glad to see you looking so relaxed, Mother," she said, bustling into the room. Inwardly, she heaved a sigh. She was going to have to remind her. Mr. Jefferson was waiting for the money.

Mrs. Bailey struggled to sit upright. Her grandsons hurried to help her.

"I thought you'd forgotten all about me," she

whispered. "I'm not staying in here a day longer, so there! I'll be home tomorrow. I don't care what that quack of a doctor of mine says."

"Good," her daughter said dutifully, sitting down. "Life's been so dull at home without you." She raised an eyebrow at the boys, who were plumping their grandmother's pillows. They were afraid to look her way, she could tell. Afraid they mightn't be able to keep their faces straight. Dull indeed! *Come on now, Grace*, she prompted herself. *You can't put it off any longer. Take a deep breath and begin.*

"Mother," she forced out, "there's something I have to talk to you about. You see, that twenty-f—"

But amazingly her mother brushed her off. "Save all that till later, Grace," she said, dismissively. "I need Henry. Where's Henry?"

"I'm right here, Grandmother." Fat stood by his grandmother's bed, bursting to tell her about his exploits with the fruit pie and how he'd won his silver dollar. But she failed to notice his excitement.

"Fetch my book, Henry," she said, patting his hand cajolingly. "I've been waiting all afternoon for you to read to me."

Then, as she sometimes did, May Bailey took them all by surprise.

"I've been thinking," she said, gazing at the

boys fondly as they settled at either side of her bed. "I've been thinking a month is too long for you boys to wait to see your mother."

The boys exchanged delighted glances, almost afraid to believe what they were hearing.

May looked over at her daughter, who sat bolt upright in her chair. "I'm afraid there are no two ways about it, Grace. You're just going to have to learn to drive."

Words failed Grace. She nodded soundlessly.

"Begin!" May Bailey ordered her grandson, tapping the book.

"'A wonderful fact to reflect upon,'" read Fat, picking up from where he had left off last time, "'that every human creature is constituted to be that profound secret and mystery to every other.'"

"No! Not that part. I told you to begin!"

"But we've already read that bit!" protested Fat.

His grandmother's hand scrabbled at the pages, turning them back till she found the right one. "Begin again!"

Obediently, Fat started over. "'It was the best of times, it was the worst of times. It was the age of wisdom, it was the age of foolishness ...'"

The Bailey mansion was shrouded in darkness when Grace and the boys pulled up in the driveway. Hub thought how wonderful it would be if their mom lived with them here. He imagined her waiting in the doorway to welcome them home, the warm lamplight spilling from behind her across the steps. He sighed. Would that dream ever, ever come true?

Fat was thinking of their mom too. He was remembering the way she'd stood up to that Savings and Loan man in the gray suit. And the cop too. She'd screamed at them both like a fishwife, he recalled with a grin. It seemed to Fat that things were never going to be easy for them. Nerves of steel, that's what they'd need, if they were ever going to survive. Fat thought of this time as a dark tunnel they were walking through. He couldn't see the end. Would there be light and safety there? He didn't know. All he knew was that they had to keep moving forward in the hope of light.

Grace pulled the key from the ignition and climbed out of the car. Standing in the driveway, she rested her hand on the warm hood. She was actually growing to like driving, she realized with wonder. Yet why should she be surprised, considering what driving had done for her? It had opened a gate to freedom. It had helped her help Honey. And, just as in her dream, it had led her to Judd. She'd danced with Judd! She closed her eyes, just for a moment, and let the memory wash over her. It might have been the first time she'd danced with him, but it wouldn't be the last— she'd make sure of that!

With a sigh of pure happiness, she grabbed the boys' hands and pulled them towards the house. "That was a nice little holiday," she said briskly. "Too bad it's over."

Fat held up his silver dollar. "Now you only owe Mr. Jefferson twenty-four dollars," he offered. "How on earth are we ever going to pay him?"

"Maybe I'll borrow the money from your Uncle Bob. Maybe I'll ask the bank for a loan." Grace rumpled his hair. "How about we worry about tomorrow tomorrow? One day at a time, boys. One day at a time."

She opened the door and they walked into the quiet house together.

WIND AT MY BACK

① LEAVING HOME

Life will never be the same. Hub and Fat knew that the Great Depression had come to their home town—their friends and neighbors are now very poor and even food seems scarce—but they didn't think it would affect them. After all, Dad did own the local hardware store. Then the bank forecloses on Jack Bailey's loan, and everything changes—fast.

Hub and Fat suddenly find themselves plunked down in the stuffy home of their dour Grandmother Bailey—who has too many rules and not enough fun. But when real tragedy strikes, Hub and Fat realize there's more at stake than just fun.

ISBN 0-00-648149-3
$5.99
trade paperback

HarperCollins*PublishersLtd*

WIND AT MY BACK

③

MY DOG PAL

It's a dream come true for Hub and Fat: they have been entrusted to "dog-sit" Pal, the town's beloved collie. Grandmother Bailey even agreed! But trouble starts brewing when Pal is accused of terrorizing the next-door neighbor's prize-winning chickens. And things go from bad to worse when Grandmother Bailey's purse disappears and guess who looks like the culprit? Pal, of course. It's up to Hub and Fat to prove his innocence, or else...

ISBN 0-00-648159-0
$5.99
trade paperback

HarperCollins*Publishers*Ltd